"*Prego! Prego!*" a man's voi...   ...is all a big mistake!"

We all turned toward the voice, and I heard Bess gasp. The man who had spoken looked like he should be in a movie. He was tall, dark, and handsome, immaculately dressed, and looked about Ned's age—he's my boyfriend. The only problem was this guy was surrounded by men and women who looked like more FBI agents.

"That's Prince Carlo Falco," Mrs. Mahoney said. "He's the mystery."

"What a mystery!" Bess said with a giggle.

George shushed her.

"The FBI was here when his private jet landed in River Heights," Mrs. Mahoney continued. "They have arrested him for stealing a priceless painting."

NANCY DREW
girl detective™

Available from Aladdin Paperbacks

NANCY DREW

girl detective ™

#15

Framed

CAROLYN KEENE

Aladdin Paperbacks

New York   London   Toronto   Sydney

✿ ALADDIN PAPERBACKS
An imprint of Simon & Schuster Children's Publishing Division
1230 Avenue of the Americas, New York, NY 10020
Copyright © 2006 by Simon & Schuster, Inc.
All rights reserved, including the right of
reproduction in whole or in part in any form.
NANCY DREW is a registered trademark of Simon & Schuster, Inc.
ALADDIN PAPERBACKS, NANCY DREW: GIRL DETECTIVE, and colophon are trademarks of Simon & Schuster, Inc.
Manufactured in the United States of America
First Aladdin Paperbacks edition January 2006
10 9 8
Library of Congress Control Number 2004117704
ISBN-13: 978-0-689-87863-3
ISBN-10: 0-689-87863-X

Contents

The Mystery Prince

Nancy! Telephone!"

"Oh, that must be somebody I've not talked to yet," I said to my two best friends, Bess Marvin and George Fayne.

Bess giggled. "Of course it's somebody you've not talked to yet, Nancy," she said. "You haven't left the room."

"I know that, Bess," I told her. "What I mean is that I'm telling everybody to use my cell number . . . because, well," I added in a whisper, "Hannah is forgetting to give me my telephone messages."

George arched an eyebrow. *"Really?"* she said. "She never forgets anything! Is something wrong?"

I shrugged. "I've talked to Dad about it a couple of

times, but he just thinks she's worried about—"

"Nancy! It's Mrs. Mahoney!" Hannah called me again. "She needs to talk to you right away!"

"Mrs. Mahoney!" I jumped up from the sofa and headed into the kitchen. "Why would she be calling me?"

"I'm sure you'll find out in just a moment," George called after me.

Mrs. Cornelius Mahoney is the wealthiest person in River Heights. I know her really well because she donates money to almost every charity project in town, and I try to help out at some of their events. But she usually didn't call me at home.

Hannah's flour-covered hand was holding out the receiver.

"Thanks," I said.

"I hope my pie crust didn't burn while I was waiting for you," Hannah said.

"Sorry," I told her.

Actually, I hoped it hadn't burned, either. Hannah's pies were the best, and I was looking forward to eating some of whatever she was baking.

"Hello, Mrs. Mahoney," I said.

"What took you so long, Nancy?" Mrs. Mahoney inquired.

Before I could even respond, Mrs. Mahoney went

on. "Never mind, dear! I have a mystery I need you to solve."

Well, Mrs. Mahoney had said the magic word. That's what I do better than anything else in life: solve mysteries. "What's happened?" I asked.

"I don't want to discuss it over the telephone, dear," Mrs. Mahoney said. "You'll need to come to the airport right away."

"The *airport*?"

"Yes. The River Heights Regional Airport," Mrs. Mahoney said. "Please hurry."

There was a click on the other end before I could get an exact location. Our airport isn't really all that huge, but it's still big enough that I didn't want to be running from gate to gate trying to find Mrs. Mahoney.

"Come on," I said to Bess and George when I got back to the living room. "We're going to see Mrs. Mahoney at the airport."

"What is she doing at the airport?" George asked.

"I don't know, but she says there's a mystery she wants me to solve," I said.

"Well, then, what are we waiting for?" Bess said. I shouted a good-bye to Hannah, and the three of us jumped into my car and headed out to the River Heights Regional Airport. A new highway got us there in under five minutes.

"This could be great," George said as I turned into the entrance. "People flying off to exotic places—there's something exciting about it."

"Maybe there's a jet waiting to take us to where the mystery is," Bess added. "I wished I had packed a small bag."

Up ahead I saw several official-looking cars. They were all black, except for one.

"I think you're getting ahead of yourselves," I told Bess and George. "Look. Chief McGinnis is here. The mystery must have happened in the airport terminal. I don't think we're going anywhere else."

"Too bad," Bess said with a sigh.

I pulled up behind Chief McGinnis's patrol car, and the three of us got out.

"Miss! You can't park here!" an attendant said. "It's—oh, Nancy Drew! I didn't recognize you."

I smiled at the man. I had no idea who he was, but he obviously knew me, probably from all the times my picture has been in the local newspaper. That happens a lot because I have a pretty good track record for solving mysteries. Of course, it doesn't hurt that James Nickerson, my boyfriend's dad, is the publisher of the *River Heights Bugle,* either.

"Thanks! Mrs. Mahoney called me," I told the man. "She needs our help."

"Go right in. They're all at Gate One, where the private jets arrive," the man said, holding the door open for us. "Why don't I just take you through security myself. That'll save you some time."

"That's a good idea," I said. I glanced quickly at the name tag pinned to his shirt. "Thanks, John."

John checked our bags and ran us through the scanner, and in a few minutes we reached Concourse A.

"You should be all right now," John said. "Mrs. Mahoney is at Gate One with the FBI."

I looked at Bess and George. George raised an eyebrow. This was getting more and more intriguing.

"You've been a great help," I told John. "I appreciate it."

"It's a pleasure to help Nancy Drew." He gave me a big grin. "You'll catch the bad guys. You always do."

The three of us waved John a good-bye and hurried down the concourse.

We passed Chief McGinnis and one of his deputies going the other way. He barely gave us a nod, so I knew he wasn't happy to see me. He considers me a rival, which is totally ridiculous. But a lot of people in River Heights don't think Chief McGinnis can find his way out of a paper bag when it comes to crime solving.

When we finally reached Gate 1, I saw Mrs.

Mahoney talking to a couple of men who really did look like they were FBI agents.

"Mrs. Mahoney!" I called.

Mrs. Mahoney looked up. "Oh, Nancy! Thank goodness you're here."

The FBI agents turned and gave us a puzzled look. When the three of us reached them, Mrs. Mahoney said, "Nancy, this is Agent Combs and this is Agent Wong. They are with the Federal Bureau of Investigation. Gentlemen, this is Nancy Drew. She'll make your lives easier, because she's never failed to solve a case yet."

Both men raised an eyebrow. I felt like I was blushing scarlet. I could only imagine what they must be thinking.

"Oh, well, I've been lucky, I guess," I said, trying to diffuse an embarrassing situation, "but if there's anything that I can do, then I most certainly—"

Bess cleared her throat, giving me a gentle poke in the back.

"Oh, I'm sorry," I said, realizing I hadn't introduced them. "This is Bess Marvin and George Fayne, my two best friends."

The agents nodded and smiled. Thank goodness, they seemed to be taking all of this in stride and weren't bothered by what some people might think of as meddling.

"It's a pleasure to meet all of you. And actually, Nancy, I know all about you," Agent Combs said. "I met your father a couple of years ago in Washington, and we exchanged notes about our daughters." He grinned. "Our Liz likes to write mysteries, so she does her crime solving on paper."

"That's cool!" I said.

"She hasn't had anything published yet, but she's had some interest," Agent Combs added. "We're keeping our fingers crossed."

"Prego! Prego!" a man's voice said. "This is all a big mistake!"

We all turned toward the voice, and I heard Bess gasp. The man who had spoken looked like he should be in a movie. He was tall, dark, and handsome, immaculately dressed, and looked about Ned's age—he's my boyfriend. The only problem was this guy was surrounded by men and women who looked like more FBI agents.

"That's Prince Carlo Falco," Mrs. Mahoney said. "He's the mystery."

"What a mystery!" Bess said with a giggle.

George shushed her.

"The FBI was here when his private jet landed in River Heights," Mrs. Mahoney continued. "They have arrested him for stealing a priceless painting."

"Really?" I said to Mrs. Mahoney.

Agent Wong nodded. "He had it with him on his jet."

"Why would he be landing in River Heights with a stolen painting?" Bess asked.

"Maybe he had a buyer for it here," George said.

I was thinking the same thing.

"No. Prince Carlo said that he was bringing it here to give to me," Mrs. Mahoney said, "but I've never seen or even heard of Prince Carlo before, so that doesn't make sense."

I looked at Agents Combs and Wong. "If you think it might help, I'd be happy to talk to Prince Carlo on behalf of Mrs. Mahoney," I said. Actually, I expected them to tell me that they had everything under control and that my help wouldn't be necessary, but I was pleasantly surprised.

"We think that would be an excellent idea, Ms. Drew," Agent Combs said. "Mrs. Mahoney specifically requested your involvement."

"Of course," I added, "if Prince Carlo reveals anything that might be—"

Agent Wong raised his hand to stop me. "We just want to get to the bottom of this, so that's all we're asking you to do," he said.

Agent Combs looked around. "There doesn't seem

to be a flight coming into Gate Two for a couple of hours, so why don't you speak with the prince there," he said. "You should have plenty of privacy."

Agent Wong walked over to where Prince Carlo was standing with the other agents, said a few words, then the two of them came back to us.

Prince Carlo looked even more handsome close up, if that was possible.

Agent Wong introduced everyone.

Prince Carlo was gracious, but I could see the confusion in his eyes. It isn't something you usually see in a guilty person. If I had had to make a decision right then, I would have said this was all a big mistake, but I know better than to make snap judgments about crimes. Dad has trained me better than that. You have to make your decisions based on evidence, and I didn't have any of that yet.

Agents Combs and Wong led us to Gate 2.

"How about those seats over there?" I suggested.

Prince Carlo nodded.

We walked to the far end of the waiting area and sat down in two seats that backed on a window where you could see the flights coming in and out. Now we were far enough away from both Agents Combs and Wong that we could talk in normal voices, without any fear of being overheard.

"Are you a lawyer, Ms. Drew?" Prince Carlo asked.

I shook my head. "My father is," I said. "Actually, Mrs. Mahoney called me here, because I'm kind of a detective, and she said this was a mystery."

Prince Carlo relaxed. "It certainly is," he said.

"Would you like to tell me about it?" I asked.

"I'm not sure," Prince Carlo said. "What if I say something that might work against me if this ever goes to trial?"

"The FBI say they just want to find out what is going on," I said. "I trust them."

Prince Carlo arched an eyebrow. "Really?" he said.

I nodded.

"Well, I want to trust you, so I guess I have to trust them," Prince Carlo said. "My great-grandmother, Princess Teresa-Maria, asked me to deliver the painting in person to Mrs. Mahoney, here in River Heights, so I told her I would."

"Why?" I asked.

"It's a thank-you for what her family did for my family during World War Two," Prince Carlo said.

I thought about that for a minute. "That was a long time ago," I said. "Do you have any idea what it was Mrs. Mahoney's family did to warrant such a gift?"

Prince Carlo shrugged. "Actually, when the reigning member of a royal family commands you to do something, Ms. Drew," he said with a smile, "you don't ask why, even if it is your great-grandmother."

I smiled back. "I've never been in that situation before, but I think I understand," I said.

"Princess Teresa-Maria hoped Mrs. Mahoney would eventually donate the painting to the art museum here in River Heights," Prince Carlo said, "so anyone who wanted to could see it."

"Prince Carlo, surely you can imagine how all of this sounds," I said. "First of all, Mrs. Mahoney doesn't know anything about this. She's never heard of you or your family, and—"

"My great-grandmother said that she had contacted Mrs. Mahoney and that Mrs. Mahoney would be expecting me," Prince Carlo said, interrupting me. "But until I arrived in River Heights, everything was supposed to be a secret because there are other members of our family who do not want this painting to be given away."

"Should I assume, then, it's worth a great deal of money?" I asked.

Prince Carlo nodded. "We may be royal, but we're what are called 'minor' royals, and none of us are really very rich compared to the kings and queens of some of the other countries in Europe."

Well, that was an incriminating comment, I thought. If Prince Carlo wasn't very rich, then what better way to get some money than to steal one of his family's paintings, sell it in the United States, then take the money back to Italy and not use it until he felt it was safe.

Was the prince telling the truth, I wondered, or was this just some incredible international scam?

2

The Italian Connection

Suddenly the solution to this seemed obvious. It was simple. "I have an idea," I said, standing up. "I think we can solve this right away."

Prince Carlo got a strange look on his face. "What do you mean?" he asked. "What are you going to do?"

"I'm going to telephone your great-grandmother in Italy," I said.

Prince Carlo jumped out of his seat. "No!" he cried.

His outburst sent Agents Combs and Wong rushing to my side with their hands reaching toward their weapons.

"Whoa!" I said to them. "It's okay. We're not having a problem here."

They lowered their hands warily and withdrew a short distance.

"I'm sorry," Prince Carlo said in a lower voice. "It's just that—"

"It's just that if we don't, you're going to look even more suspicious than you already do," I said, interrupting him. "Why don't you want me to call her?"

Prince Carlo took a deep breath. "She isn't well," he said. "This might kill her."

I was trying to decide if he was telling the truth.

"Why would you think that?" I asked.

"I'm her favorite," Prince Carlo said, a blush spreading across his face. "If she thought I might be going to jail, it could put so much stress on her heart that, well . . ."

He stopped and I could see the tears in his eyes. Was he playing me or were those real tears? I wondered. "You're in a real mess here, Prince Carlo, and if you don't like my idea, I hope you have one that's better."

"I do," Prince Carlo said.

"Let's hear it then."

"Princess Teresa-Maria never answers the telephone," Prince Carlo said. "You have to talk to Giovanna before you can talk to my great-grandmother."

"Who's Giovanna?" I asked.

"She's my grandmother's secretary, helper, and confidante," Prince Carlo replied. "My great-grandmother trusts her completely."

"What about you?" I asked. "Do you trust her?"

"Of course," Prince Carlo said. "She was my nanny, too."

"You're sure she hasn't sided with some of your other relatives?" I questioned him.

"Never!" Prince Carlo said.

"Okay, then, we'll talk to Giovanna first." I nodded my head toward Agents Combs and Wong. "We need to do this with the FBI listening, though, or it won't do much good."

"All right," Prince Carlo agreed.

"I think we can resolve this," I called to Agents Combs and Wong.

The two FBI agents walked over to us.

"Let's hear your plan," Agent Combs said.

He didn't sound too enthusiastic. I wondered if maybe they had had second thoughts about letting me get involved.

"We're going to telephone Prince Carlo's great-grandmother, Princess Teresa-Maria in Italy," I explained. "She'll corroborate his story."

Both agents looked a little skeptical.

"This is what I was trying to tell your other agents," Prince Carlo said, "but nobody would listen to me."

"We have to talk to Giovanna first, though," I said.

"Who's Giovanna?" Agent Wong asked.

Prince Carlo repeated the description he had given me earlier.

"How do we know this isn't some sort of a setup?" Agent Combs asked. "You could have prearranged this with Giovanna. You could have coached her about what to say in case you got caught."

Now I could see anger in Prince Carlo's eyes. "Forgive me, but I'm not used to having people so suspicious of me," he managed to say. "I come from a very old, very proud Italian family, and if you would just hear me out, then maybe we could—"

"Look, Prince Carlo," Agent Combs said, interrupting him. "You have to understand where we're coming from too. The Italian authorities asked us to meet your jet when it landed here in River Heights. They said you might have a very rare painting with you that you had stolen from the family. You did. All I'm saying is that you might not be working alone. You could have other people helping you. It wouldn't be the first time. We can't just take your word for this."

"We wouldn't be doing our jobs, if we did that," Agent Wong added.

Prince Carlo let out a heavy sigh, but he didn't say anything.

"You told me you thought I might be able to help solve this mystery," I told the two agents. "Well, I think we need to hear what Prince Carlo has to say."

"Okay, we'll give him five minutes," Agent Combs said.

Prince Carlo took a deep breath. "All right. As I told Ms. Drew, I—"

"Please call me Nancy," I told him.

I could see Agent Combs almost biting his tongue to keep from saying something.

"Okay. As I told *Nancy,* Giovanna answers my great-grandmother's telephone, so we'd have to go through her first, and there's only one thing that will get my grandmother to the telephone, and that's to talk to a journalist doing a story on Italian royalty."

"Why?" Agent Wong asked.

"Princess Teresa–Maria lives for the return of the Italian monarch to the throne," Prince Carlo said. "She thinks if people keep reading positive articles about the royals in the newspapers, then it might happen one day."

"Really?" I said.

Prince Carlo nodded. "Who knows? A lot of Italians get tired of politics and politicians," he said. "They think it would be a good idea."

"So how is this going to help you out?" Agent Combs asked, bringing us back to the present.

"Well, if Nancy tells Giovanna that she's a reporter doing a story on Italian royalty for an American newspaper, I guarantee that my grandmother will talk to her."

Now, I was getting it! "And if I identify myself as a reporter for the *River Heights Bugle* and tell Princess Teresa-Maria that I'm calling—because her great-grandson is here in River Heights to deliver a famous painting to Mrs. Mahoney—then we'll have our corroboration."

"Or not," Agent Wong added.

"Or not," I reluctantly agreed.

"We'll let you do this on two conditions," Agent Combs said. "We get to make sure that the number you're calling actually belongs to Princess Teresa-Maria, and you'll make the call on our equipment, so we can listen in."

"I don't have any problem with that," Prince Carlo said. "I'm telling the truth."

While we waited for the FBI to set up the telephone equipment I'd be using, I thought about what

I would tell Giovanna. When Agent Combs finally signaled that they were ready for me, I had my story down pat.

I sat down in one of the seats in the Gate 1 waiting area and picked up the receiver. Another FBI agent dialed the number in Italy. I thought the clicks would never end. Finally a voice on the other end said, *"Pronto!"*

Suddenly I panicked. How dumb could we be! Of course Giovanna would answer in Italian. I only knew a few words. Before I could open my mouth, Prince Carlo realized what had happened and whispered, "She speaks English fluently."

Immediately I went into my routine. "Hello! My name's Nancy Drew, and I'm calling from River Heights in the United States." I stopped and waited.

"Yes. What may I do for you?"

Prince Carlo was right. Giovanna's English was flawless, with just a slight accent.

I immediately launched into why I wanted to talk to Princess Teresa-Maria.

"Oh, I am so glad you called!" Giovanna said. "Is Prince Carlo there with you?"

"Uh, well, uh . . ." I looked at the agents around me. "I'm sorry. The connection isn't very good. Would you please repeat what you just said, and slowly?"

While Giovanna was repeating her question, I looked up to see how I should answer it.

"Tell her he's in the area," Agent Wong said.

"He's in the area," I repeated, wondering if that would make sense to her. "Why do you ask?"

"I need to get a message to him," Giovanna said. "It's very important."

I put my hand over the receiver and looked at Prince Carlo. "She says she needs to get an important message to you," I told him in a whisper.

Prince Carlo's face darkened. "Let me talk to her!" he said.

"No!" Agent Combs objected.

Prince Carlo ignored him and took the receiver out of my hands. *"Giovanna! Ecco Carlo!"* he said in Italian. "What's wrong?"

With a flick of a switch, the telephone was on speaker, so everyone could now hear what Giovanna was saying.

"Where are you, my dear boy? Princess Teresa-Maria took a turn for the worse," Giovanna said, her voice choked by sobs. "She's been taken to a hospital in Milan. You must go to her at once."

"I can't, Giovanna—I'm out of the country," Prince Carlo said, "but I will get there as soon as possible. Tell her that I love her and that I've fulfilled her wish."

20

"I shall, dear Carlo," Giovanna said. *"Arrivederci!"*

The FBI ended the connection.

Prince Carlo's face was ashen.

"So even Giovanna doesn't know why you are here?" I said.

Prince Carlo shook his head. "Princess Teresa-Maria didn't want to get her involved," he said.

I knew what he was thinking. If Princess Teresa-Maria died, then there would be no one to corroborate his story about the painting, and he could spend several years in prison.

3

Royal Intrigues

Prince Carlo looked at me with his movie-star dark brown eyes. "*Per piacere,* Nancy," he said. "You have to make them believe me. I've been framed by other members of my family."

The FBI agents had now gathered together in a single group, several yards away from us, and were, I was sure, discussing what their next move would be. From overhearing bits of their conversation, I knew they wanted to make certain they did the right thing to avoid an international incident. I hoped that would give me time to put my own plan into play.

"You need a good lawyer," I told Prince Carlo. "I know just the one to call."

I quickly dialed Dad's law office number on my

cell phone. His secretary answered and said he was in an important meeting, but when I told her it was an emergency, she put me through right away.

"Nancy?" Dad said. "Has something happened?"

Dad's voice was full of concern. Ever since my mother died, when I was just three years old, he's handled both roles—and very well, too—but I know that some of my mystery-solving adventures have given him a few gray hairs.

"Yes, but not to me, Dad." I quickly told him what was going on. "Prince Carlo needs a good lawyer, and he needs one now."

"I'll be right there," Dad said. "My meeting was just ending."

When I looked around, Agents Combs and Wong were talking to Prince Carlo. I joined them.

"I just called my father," I told them. "He's agreed to represent Prince Carlo."

Both agents seemed relieved. Now they didn't have to make a decision that might get them in trouble.

"We'll leave you two together, then, until your father gets here," Agent Wong said.

Prince Carlo and I walked back to where we had been sitting to wait for Dad to arrive. When he finally got there, I could tell that he had literally run through the airport, because he was out of breath.

"This is my father, Carson Drew," I told Prince Carlo. "I'm bragging, I know, but you're in very good hands."

Dad and Prince Carlo shook hands.

"I'll be right back," Dad said.

Prince Carlo watched as Dad went over and spoke to Agents Combs and Wong. They nodded a couple of times, then the three of them shook hands.

I could see on Prince Carlo's face that this seemed a little suspicious, so I said, "My father has worked with the FBI before. Don't worry."

Prince Carlo nodded, but he didn't say anything.

When Dad got back to us, he said, "Things are better than I thought they were, Prince Carlo. Our government wants to get to the bottom of this, of course, but I just found out that there have been telephone calls from the Italian ambassador and a couple of other dignitaries in support of you, and so our authorities want to make sure they don't upset our Italian friends."

I looked at Prince Carlo. "That's a good sign," I said.

He nodded, and I thought I saw the beginning of a smile.

"Let's sit and talk," Dad said. "I know you've

probably already covered this with Nancy, but I need to hear it myself."

Prince Carlo started at the beginning, with how Princess Teresa-Maria had wanted to repay Mrs. Mahoney's family for their help during World War II.

I looked over and waved to Bess and George. They had been sitting patiently in another one of the waiting areas. Now a couple of the FBI agents had joined them. Bess was chatting with one of the agents, while George was pointing out something on her laptop to the other one. I don't know anybody who knows as much about computers as George does.

When Prince Carlo finished the part of his story that I had already heard and began adding new details, I refocused on what he was saying.

"There's a power struggle in my family," Prince Carlo said. "My great-grandmother, Princess Teresa-Maria, is the head now, but she wants me to be in charge after she dies. Of course that means several people would be bypassed, and that's not sitting well with certain members of the family."

"What does it really mean, Prince Carlo, if these other members are passed over?" Dad asked.

"Nothing, really. It's mostly about status," Prince Carlo said.

"Then why all the fuss?" Dad asked.

"It's a European mind-set," Prince Carlo said. "Many people still long for the days of monarchy, and that's what my family represents."

"They see your family as a return to the glory days of their history," I said. "Right?"

Prince Carlo nodded. "They remember only the glamorous things about monarchy," he said. "They don't remember any of the bad. Americans might find that hard to understand."

"Oh, I think Americans do understand," Dad said. "A lot of people in this country are really fascinated by royalty."

I nodded. "Look at how popular Princess Diana was," I said.

"How does this all fit in with what's happening to you now, though?" Dad asked.

"Well, the painting I brought to Mrs. Mahoney is worth a lot of money, so that would be some of it, of course," Prince Carlo said. "But there are certain members of my family, the ones my great-grandmother wants to pass over, who have been trying to create problems for me for years."

"If you were in prison or if you were involved in something scandalous, something that would hurt your family's name, then it would be hard for your

26

great-grandmother to justify naming you head," I said. "Is that it?"

Prince Carlo nodded. "Exactly. They couldn't have asked for anything more perfect to fit their plans than this."

"Tell me more about why Princess Teresa-Maria wanted to give Mrs. Mahoney the painting," Dad said. "Why doesn't your family think this is a good idea?"

"I think I must be the only one in my family who actually believes my great-grandmother," Prince Carlo said. "Almost everyone else thinks it's just a fantasy concocted by a frail mind."

"You mean they don't believe someone in Mrs. Mahoney's family actually did what Princess Teresa-Maria said they did?" I asked.

Prince Carlo nodded. "I'm not even sure I actually believe it either," he admitted. "It's just that . . . well, I love my great-grandmother, and it's just not within me to question her or her motives. Maybe I simply didn't want to accept that she might not be in touch with reality."

"It's hard to deal with things like that with someone you love dearly." Dad looked at me.

My heart skipped a beat. I knew Dad was thinking about Hannah, and all of a sudden I could identify with how Prince Carlo felt. I simply couldn't imagine a time when Hannah's mental capacity would be diminished and she wouldn't be able to do all the things both Dad and I counted on her to do.

Suddenly I thought of something else. "Is there anyone else who might know about what happened during World War Two to make Princess Teresa-Maria donate this painting to Mrs. Mahoney's family?" I asked Prince Carlo.

"I asked my great-grandmother the same question, Nancy. There isn't anyone else," Prince Carlo said. "Everyone in Italy who was involved in helping save our family fortune is dead: my great-grandfather, their servants, everyone."

"Your great-grandmother never mentioned who it was in Mrs. Mahoney's family who did this deed?" Dad asked.

Prince Carlo shook his head. "Never," he said.

"I guess this is why Mrs. Mahoney called me, Dad," I said. "This is the mystery she wants me to solve."

Dad nodded. "I can take care of the legal aspects of the case, Prince Carlo," he said. "Nancy handles the mystery solving."

"I hope she can solve this one," Prince Carlo said.

"As much as I like this country, I don't want to spend any time in one of its prisons."

I had a good feeling about Prince Carlo. For some reason, I just believed he was telling the truth, but I knew I had to come up with solid evidence to present to the authorities.

"We'll try to make sure that doesn't happen," I told him.

4

House Arrest!

I heard a gurgling noise and suddenly realized it was Prince Carlo's stomach.

I wondered what the royal protocol was for that. Did you pretend not to hear it? Did you say you were hungry and ask if he might be hungry too?

Fortunately Prince Carlo didn't seem embarrassed, because he said, "I think my stomach is trying to tell me something."

"I bet you're starved," I said. "When was the last time you ate?"

"Last night before I left," Prince Carlo replied.

Out of the corner of one eye I saw Bess and George headed in our direction. I was sure I was going to hear from them about being abandoned, but Bess only said, "We're going to get something to eat. Does anybody want anything?"

"You've got great timing," Prince Carlo said. He offered his hand to them. "You must be Nancy's friends. I'm Carlo Falco."

George smiled and shook his hand. "I'm George."

Prince Carlo nodded and turned to Bess, pausing over her hand a little longer than usual. Men are always attracted to Bess, and it looked like princes are no exception.

"It is such a pleasure to meet you," Bess said. "I've read all about you, and I've seen you on television, in one of those celebrity confidential shows."

Prince Carlo grinned. "Well, I hope you didn't believe everything they said about me," he said.

"Oh, it wasn't anything bad at all." Bess said. "They were just talking about jet-setting European royalty."

"Well, there are people who are better at that than I am."

Prince Carlo's stomach grumbled again, and it was Bess and George's turn to wonder what to say.

"I told you your timing was great," Prince Carlo said. "I'm famished."

"He hasn't eaten since last night in Italy," I told

them. I looked at Dad. "Do you think it would be all right if the four of us went to one of the food courts?"

"I think Prince Carlo should stay here with me, Nancy," Dad said. "It would be better if you brought the food to him. I don't want the FBI to think we're trying to circumvent our agreement."

"All right." I turned to Prince Carlo. "What are you hungry for?"

"Anything is fine," he said. "I'll take whatever you three think looks good."

"Okay," I said.

The three of us started toward a food court I had seen on the way down to Gate 1.

"Oh, he is absolutely, totally gorgeous," Bess said when we were out of hearing. "I thought you had planned to keep him all to yourself."

"Please! I don't think Ned would appreciate that," I told them. "Anyway, he's not my type."

"You don't think *Princess Nancy* sounds good?" Bess teased. "I think *Princess Bess* does."

"You can keep your royal titles," George said. "Just give me a hamburger and some fries, and I'll be satisfied."

"I'm with you," I said.

Bess stopped. "Well, if you think I'm going to

invite you to my coronation with that attitude, you're sadly mistaken," she said.

I looked at her. "Are you serious?" I asked.

"Of course not," Bess said, "but you have to admit that it's kind of a once-in-a-lifetime experience, getting to meet a real prince."

"He seems like an ordinary guy," George said.

"I know. That's what makes this so difficult," I said. "I want to believe he's innocent, because he is so nice, but I can't make any judgments until I've examined the evidence."

We were close enough to the food court that the various aromas started assaulting our noses.

"The shortest line is at Hamburger Haven," I said. "Is that okay?"

"It's fine with me," George said. "That's what I wanted in the first place."

"I think I'll get a chicken salad sandwich at the French Café," Bess said. "They're pretty fast too."

"Okay, but if you're still in line when we get our hamburgers, we'll go on back to Prince Carlo," I said. "He really must be starving."

"Okay," Bess said.

As it turned out, Bess got her order several minutes before we got ours, so the three of us went back to the gate together.

Prince Carlo and Dad seemed to be sharing a joke when we walked up. I was glad Prince Carlo was beginning to relax.

I handed him his hamburger and fries, and for the next several minutes, we just ate.

"I love American fast food," Prince Carlo said between bites. "What an invention!"

"I guess it sort of fits our lifestyle," I told him, "but a lot of Americans also like to linger over a well-cooked meal."

We had just finished eating when Agents Combs and Wong walked up.

"It's all been arranged, Mr. Drew," Agent Wong said. "Your name moves mountains in Washington."

"What's been arranged?" I asked.

"Prince Carlo is being released into your father's custody, without bail," Agent Combs said, "but he'll be under house arrest and can only travel in the company of Mr. Drew."

Agent Wong looked at Prince Carlo. "You have a good friend in the Italian ambassador," he said. "He believes you're innocent."

"I am," Prince Carlo insisted.

Agents Combs and Wong didn't say anything.

Agent Combs handed Dad a card. "If you need to

reach us, this is the number to call," he said. "It'll be answered twenty-four hours a day."

"Thank you," Dad said. "I don't anticipate any problems, though."

"We've removed Prince Carlo's suitcase from his jet," Agent Wong said. "We've searched it, so it can be released. One of our agents has it in front of the terminal, where you can pick it up on your way out."

"All right." Dad turned to us. "Ready?"

We all nodded.

As we headed back down Concourse A toward the exit, I wondered what the next few days would bring in the way of revelations about Prince Carlo and the priceless painting.

5

Paparazzi

We left the terminal and headed for the parking lot, Prince Carlo and Dad getting into his car, which was parked just down from mine. "I wonder if one of us should ride with your father," Bess said. "After all, we wouldn't want Prince Carlo to think we were stuck up or anything."

George laughed. "Yeah, right!" she said. "Are you volunteering yourself, Cousin?"

Bess grinned. "Well, if somebody's got to do it, it might as well be me," she said.

"Nobody has to do anything," I told them. "Anyway, I'm sure Prince Carlo and Dad need to talk about his case in private, lawyer to client."

"That's a good point." Bess sighed. "I was only kidding anyway."

We got into my car, followed Dad to where we paid our parking fee, then left the airport and headed back toward my house.

"What did Prince Carlo tell you about his jet, Nancy?" George asked. "I want to know about it, and don't leave out any details. I'm especially interested in the jet's computer system."

"Computer systems were the last thing on his mind, George," I told her. "We only talked about the mess he's in."

George shook her head in dismay. "How can computers be the last thing on anyone's mind?"

"Oh, George! There's a prince in town and you want to know about computers!" Bess exclaimed. "I want to know about Italy." She looked over at me. "You do know that George and I will be spending more time than usual at your place. Are you up to it?"

"Of course I'm up to it," I said. "Anyway, I'm sure I'll need you two to help me with the case."

"I don't believe for a minute that he's guilty," Bess said.

"Oh, Bess, you say that about everybody," George chimed in.

It was true. It was almost impossible for Bess to understand how anybody could be bad. She had an explanation for everyone's behavior that always gave him or her the benefit of the doubt.

As we headed home, I kept Dad's car in sight. I doubted Prince Carlo would grab the steering wheel, force Dad out of the car, and then take off for parts unknown. I guess, though, it's just part of being a detective, even an amateur one, to be a little suspicious until innocence is proven.

I had just finished telling Bess and George everything that I thought I could without betraying confidences when we turned onto our street.

"Watch out, Nancy!" George cried.

Up ahead Dad's car was stopped in the middle of the street, and for just a minute I wondered if Prince Carlo had actually bolted, but then I saw why Dad wasn't moving. There were two vans with satellite dishes on top of them parked in front of our house. Our yard was covered with people milling around.

"What on earth is going on?" Bess asked.

"Oh, no!" I cried. "I wonder if something has happened to Hannah!"

"You did say she was acting kind of strange lately, didn't you?" Bess said.

"Not strange, just forgetful," I told her. "Maybe she . . ." I stopped. "No, if something had happened to her, there would be police cars or an ambulance, not television vans, and I don't see any of those around."

"You're right," George agreed. "It has to be something else."

"Paparazzi!" I said. "Word must have gotten out somehow that Prince Carlo is in River Heights, and they're trying to get whatever pictures they can. I wonder how they found out he'd be here, though."

"Whoever told them, they sure got here fast," George said.

"Can you imagine having to deal with this every day of your life?" Bess said.

"No, I can't," I said.

Through the rear window of Dad's car, I could see him punching in numbers on his cell phone.

Within seconds my phone was ringing.

"Dad?" I answered.

"Nancy, I'm calling Chief McGinnis to clear the street so we can drive into the garage," Dad told me. "As soon as he does that, we'll both pull into the garage, and I'll shut the doors before we get out, okay?"

"Okay," I said.

I gave Bess and George the gist of the conversation.

"Actually, I think I'd like to work the crowd," George said. "I'd like to find out the psychological reason why people do things like this."

We only had to wait about five minutes before three River Heights police cars showed up. Chief McGinnis was in the lead. He actually waved when he passed. I was glad to see that he wasn't angry at being forced out of the picture by the FBI at the airport.

Of course, I did think the flashing lights and sirens were a bit over the top, but it helped to clear the street enough that Dad and I could pull into the driveway and then into the garage.

When the garage door was back down, we all got out of our cars. Prince Carlo grabbed his suitcase. For just a moment I thought about offering to carry it, thinking that royalty should never carry their own bags, but then I decided that would be ridiculous— and probably embarrassing for him.

Hannah was standing at the door that led into the kitchen. "What in the world is going on?" she said. "I've never seen anything like this!" Then she noticed Prince Carlo. "Nobody told me we'd be having company for dinner."

"Hannah, this is Prince Carlo Falco from Italy," I told her.

Prince Carlo smiled, approached Hannah, took her hand and kissed it, just like I had seen people do in the movies. I wished I had my camera to capture the look on Hannah's face.

A flustered Hannah said, "Well, it's no problem, really, and, well, if you'll excuse me, I'll go set an extra plate."

Even though it was several hours before we would eat, I said, "Set *three* more, Hannah. Bess and George will be staying for dinner too."

Smiles erupted on my friends' faces.

Dad led the way inside our house. "I'm sorry for the circus atmosphere outside, Prince Carlo," he said. "I suppose you have to endure this in Italy all the time."

"Unfortunately," Prince Carlo said. "Our family is just minor royalty, but that doesn't seem to matter."

"I think they need to get a life," George said.

"George!" Bess exclaimed.

Prince Carlo laughed. "No, no, no, it's all right," he said. "George is right."

"I'll show you the guest room, Prince Carlo," Dad said.

"That would be wonderful." Prince Carlo turned to us. "I know I'll see you all later, but I just want to thank you for helping me out. I don't know what I would have done without you."

"We're not through yet," I reminded him. "I'm going to prove you're innocent."

"I have no doubt you will," Prince Carlo said.

With that, he and Dad started upstairs to the guest room.

"Oh, that was dumb!" I said, berating myself.

"What was dumb?" George asked.

"You don't treat suspects like that," I said. "You don't tell them that you're going to prove their innocence. I'm a detective, not a lawyer. You just tell them you're going to do your best to find out the facts in the case."

"I think he's innocent," Bess said.

"Yes, yes, we know," I told her. "We've been through this before."

"Don't you think he's innocent?" George asked.

"I don't know what to believe," I replied. "He's so nice, and he seems innocent, but I have to keep an open mind."

"I know what you mean," Bess said. "Don't worry, we'll help."

Outside, it seemed that the crowd was getting noisier. I walked over to the window and looked out.

"I thought they'd all be gone by now," I said. "I don't see Chief McGinnis or the other deputies anywhere."

"I'm not quite sure you can keep people from gathering like this," George said. "If they're not disturbing the peace, and if they're not actually standing on your property, and if they're not creating a hazard, like blocking the street, then, well, I think you just have to deal with it."

"There's a reporter talking to people in the crowd," I said. "I wonder what she's asking them."

"Why are you here? What would you do if you married Prince Carlo and went to live in Italy?" Bess said. "Stuff like that."

"Oh, that is so dumb," George said.

"I think so too," I agreed. "I think she needs to talk to somebody who knows what's going on."

"Well, there are three of us here," Bess said. "Are you suggesting that we go outside and give her the real scoop?"

I thought about that for a minute. "Well, at least they'd know the truth, and I think that's important," I said. "And then we'd be sure they got the story right."

"I'm game," Bess said. "I think it would be kind of fun."

"Okay, we'll do it," I said, "but we're not to give away any confidential information."

"Okay," Bess and George agreed.

The three of us walked to the front door, and I opened it slowly, but evidently not slowly enough, because we were immediately rushed by the crowd.

All of a sudden there were microphones in front of all three of us.

I recognized the woman standing right in front of me. She anchored the morning news on my favorite River Heights television station.

"Nancy, how long have you known Prince Carlo?" she asked.

"Just a few hours," I replied.

"So you're not engaged to him?" she asked, disappointment showing in her voice.

"What?" I said. "Would you repeat that?"

"We understand that Prince Carlo arrived here to propose to you," the woman explained, "and after you're married, you'll return to Italy, where you'll be living in his castle."

Could these people be any more out of touch with reality? "No! That's not true at all!" I said. "I hate to disappoint you, but here's the real story."

The crowd was suddenly quiet, all of them turned to me with expectant looks on their faces. I could see out of the corner of my eye that both Bess and George looked a little peeved that their interviews had been terminated.

For the next ten minutes I gave them Prince Carlo's story, at least as much of it as I thought I could reveal. Unfortunately that made them even more intrigued than my impending wedding.

"The Prince of Thieves!" someone in the crowd shouted.

"Robin Hood! Right!" someone else shouted. "Prince Carlo robs from his rich family to give to the poor!"

"Except that Mrs. Mahoney isn't poor," the first person said. "What's wrong with this picture?"

That brought some snickers from the crowd.

This had gone far enough, I decided. I stepped past the anchorwoman and stood at the edge of our porch. "As I'm sure you can all understand, Prince Carlo is tired and would like to get some rest," I said. "River Heights is known for the hospitality it always offers its visitors, so my father and I would appreciate it if you would—"

"He's not a guest!" someone shouted. "He's a crook!"

"No, he's not!" someone else shouted. "He's a very nice man!"

"How do you know?"

"I think he's cute!"

"What do you know?"

I stepped back. Obviously my request had fallen on deaf ears, as the crowd continued to shout back and forth.

Just then Chief McGinnis and two deputies arrived again with their sirens blaring and lights flashing. The crowd backed away from the house.

Chief McGinnis pulled into our driveway and got out. "All right, folks, I told you about crowding the Drews' house!" he shouted. "I don't want to have to arrest anybody, but you have to back off."

For once I was glad Chief McGinnis was on the scene. The crowd actually seemed to be paying attention to him. From the look on his face, I think it surprised even him.

He nodded to us from the driveway, then got back into his car, and backed out. One of the other deputies followed him, but the third one stayed where he was, parked across the street. I was glad that we'd have someone handling the crowd control.

A couple of the reporters acted as if they wanted to talk to me some more, but I gave them a big smile as I opened the front door, so Bess, George, and I could go back inside.

Hannah was standing on the other side of the living room, hands on her hips. "I called the police," she said. "This is terrible."

"I know it is, Hannah," I said, "but it's what you expect when there's a celebrity crime."

Actually, that was the first time I had even thought about this case that way—a celebrity crime. I had certainly seen them on television before, but I had never expected to be a part of one.

Just then Prince Carlo came downstairs. He had changed into more comfortable clothes.

"You did a wonderful job handling that crowd, Nancy," Prince Carlo said. "I was watching you from the upstairs window."

"You wouldn't believe what they thought was happening," George said. "They thought you had come here to marry Nancy."

I could feel myself turning scarlet. "Well, that just goes to show you how far off the news can be," I managed to say.

Prince Carlo gave me a big grin. "That wouldn't be such a terrible thing, but I know Nancy's taken," he said. "While you were outside, your friend Ned called. He's on his way over here from the university."

Ned, I thought. I was happy to hear that. We were each other's support. Just thinking about Ned made me feel more grounded. Normally whenever I'm working on a case, the mystery is the focus, but now, with Prince Carlo, I had the mystery to solve and the press to deal with too. How distracting would the circus outside our house be? If I was going to solve the mystery of why an Italian princess would donate a painting worth big money to a woman she'd never met, then I had to stay focused, and I knew that was going to be hard to do.

6

Stressed Out!

Over the next few days we were eventually able to settle into a routine of sorts. Dad was busy getting together his arguments to prove that Prince Carlo was innocent, and I was, well, trying to figure out exactly what I was going to do to solve this mystery. I can tell you right off that I was beginning to feel the pressure. That's the problem when you're sort of famous in your hometown. It seems like nobody thinks there is a mystery that I couldn't possibly solve, but it's not always easy in the beginning trying to figure out what the first step is.

I don't know what I expected, but Prince Carlo was not a demanding guest. I suppose I had seen too many movies where royalty expected to be waited on hand and foot. That's certainly not what happened with Prince Carlo. In fact, he actually helped Hannah in the kitchen, spent hours answering Bess and George's questions, and even turned out to be better than a library for Ned, who was working on a paper about Italian literature of the twentieth century.

We still had to deal with the press and paparazzi in front of our house, but even that was manageable. A couple of times a day I'd go outside and, like a press agent, give whoever was there a briefing about Prince Carlo. He and I had worked out ahead of time the things to say that he thought would satisfy the crowd, and he was right. It was mostly minor stuff, like what he'd had for breakfast, what American television programs he found interesting, and what he was wearing that day. Of course, there were always people in the crowd who weren't satisfied and who wanted to hear from the prince in person, but I told them that was impossible, given his current circumstances. They grumbled, but no one tried to storm the house.

Then the worst happened! One morning we woke up to a smoke alarm, and Dad and I found Hannah in the kitchen, staring into space while the toast burned in the toaster and the bacon scorched in the frying pan. Dad decided to call an ambulance, thinking it would be faster and that it might scatter the crowd in front of our house. We had to put Hannah in the hospital.

When we finally got to talk to the doctors, they said they wanted to do a battery of tests on her. Fortunately River Heights has a great hospital, but "a battery" didn't sound good. Dad kept telling me not to worry, but I couldn't help it, especially when I could tell he was worried too. They kept her sedated to keep her calm during the tests, so she didn't really know what was going on.

The doctors and nurses assured us that there was nothing we could do, that we'd just be in the way if we hung around the hospital. They said they'd notify us if there was any change, but we still checked in on her a couple of times a day, and even snuck in a couple of late-night visits. I don't know what either Dad or I would do if anything happened to Hannah.

Now I was doing my best not only to run the household, which included cooking—or microwaving—but also to deal with the crowds in front of the house and to keep up Prince Carlo's spirits. Not to mention the mystery I was supposed to be solving. And Hannah was never far from my mind.

I had just come in from one of my "briefings" with the press when Prince Carlo met me in the living room.

"I have a big favor to ask of you, Nancy," he said.

"Ask away," I told him.

"At home, I paint whenever I can. It relaxes me and I really enjoy it," Prince Carlo said. "Naturally, I didn't think I'd be in America this long, so I didn't bring any supplies with me. Do you think you'd be able to . . ." His voice trailed off. "Oh, that's asking too much of you."

"No, it's not," I replied quickly. "I wouldn't mind getting you whatever you needed." I hesitated. "You're not talking about painting our house, are you?"

Prince Carlo laughed. "That's a good one," he said. "No, no, I'm talking about the paints and canvas that an artist uses."

"Is this just a hobby?" I asked, fascinated to learn about this new side of Prince Carlo. "Have you ever had any art shows?"

"Well, it certainly started out as a hobby, but it soon turned into a very lucrative sideline," Prince Carlo replied. "Of course, at first, I thought people were only buying my paintings because of who I am, but when I started to do shows, my work was reviewed by art critics, and for the most part, their comments have been very positive."

"That is so exciting!" I said. I looked at my watch. "I could do that right now. I don't like to be bored either. It won't take me but just a few minutes. I know exactly where to go."

"Oh, thank you, Nancy!" Prince Carlo said. "I didn't want to admit this, because it sounds so, well, like I'm a whiner—is that the word? But I am about to lose my mind without something to do."

I called Bess and George and told them to meet me at the River Heights Art Gallery. It was a relatively new place, but I had been in there several times, looking for paintings that I thought Dad would like in his redecorated law office and buying art supplies in the attached small but well-stocked shop. I had even found a painting that I thought Hannah might like in her bedroom. I certainly don't know a whole lot about art, but I do know what I like. Fortunately my choices were a big hit.

"Do you think the gallery would take my credit card, Nancy?" Prince Carlo asked. "I'll give it to you, and if there's a problem—"

"Oh, just let me take care of this now, and you can pay me back later," I told him. "It's nothing I'm worried about."

"Well, thanks, Nancy. You're a lifesaver." Prince Carlo handed me a list. "These are the things I need. They're pretty ordinary, so there should be no problem getting them."

"Okay," I said. "I'll be back in a little while."

I guess that I had talked myself into believing that I could leave the house unnoticed, but that was really dumb on my part. It took me several minutes to back out of the driveway because people crowded around my car, peering in the windows to see if Prince Carlo was inside. Several of them even tried to open the doors. Finally I made it to the street, but for the first half block I had people running alongside me. I never knew when Chief McGinnis or his deputies would be parked outside our house. Naturally, when they needed to be there, they weren't, and when they really weren't needed, they were. Luckily, when I reached the end of the block, they all gave up and started back toward the front of our house.

Bess and George were already inside the gallery when I got there. The owner, Jocylin Ross, was showing them around. She waved when I entered.

"It's good to see you, Nancy," Jocylin said, extending her hand when I walked up. "I've been wondering how things were at your house. I've seen you on television several times. Imagine! Playing host to an Italian prince!"

"Aunt Jocylin?"

We all turned toward the voice that had come from the back of the gallery. It must have been the light, but the girl I saw looked like a painting come alive.

"Sophia, come here, dear," Jocylin called to her. "I want you to meet Nancy Drew and her friends."

Sophia literally seemed to float toward us, she was so ethereal, and offered us a perfectly sculpted porcelain hand.

"Sophia was reared in Italy, so she speaks fluent Italian," Jocylin explained, which accounted for the slight accent I had detected. "Her parents, my sister and her husband, went there to live right after she was born. They had an art gallery in Rome. They sold mostly paintings by Americans living in Italy."

"They were killed in an avalanche last year," Sophia said. "Aunt Jocylin wanted me to come live here in River Heights with her. I was so glad she did."

"Do you paint?" Bess asked.

"Yes, I do." Sophia's eyes had brightened. "Would you like to see some of my work?"

"Definitely!" the three of us said in unison, then laughed.

I handed Jocylin Prince Carlo's list. "Our guest is a painter, and he's wanting to keep his mind occupied," I said. "These are the things he's asked me to pick up. I hope you have them."

Jocylin gave the list a quick glance. "I think we have everything in stock," she said. "I'll have it ready for you when Sophia gets through with her private showing."

I wasn't exactly sure what I had expected from Sophia's paintings—maybe something more amateurish—but once we were in her small studio, I had the feeling we were in one of the world's major art galleries. For almost half an hour we admired and discussed her work, completely losing track of time. I felt a little bad since I knew Prince Carlo was waiting for his art supplies.

"I am so impressed, Sophia," I told her as we started back toward the front of the gallery.

"Are any of them for sale?" Bess asked.

Sophia's face clouded. "That's not why I—"

"Oh, I'm sorry. I didn't mean to give you the impression that I thought that's why you showed us your paintings," Bess said hurriedly. "In fact, I'm a very hard sell, so if I don't want to buy something, then no amount of pressure can get me to do it. But I really love your work. I've never seen anything like it."

The smile returned to Sophia's face. "Let me think about which ones I might want to give up." She shook her head in dismay. "I'll probably never be a successful artist because I can't stand the thought of parting with any of my work. I grow so close to each painting."

"I can only imagine," George said.

Jocylin had Prince Carlo's materials ready, so I paid for them, then invited Bess and George to come to my house later for dinner. After seeing Sophia's work, Bess had hinted strongly that she'd like to talk to Prince Carlo about his paintings. After saying good-bye to my friends and thanking Jocylin and Sophia, I headed home.

Pulling into my driveway was "déjà vu all over again," as Yogi Berra would say, until I was safely inside the garage. Dad and Prince Carlo were sitting in the living room going over some business, but when Prince Carlo saw me and the bag in my hand, he brightened.

"You're a lifesaver, Nancy," Prince Carlo said.

"What's this?" Dad asked.

I explained where I had been and what I had done. "I'll put this all in your room," I said. "You and Dad go ahead and finish what you were talking about."

"Well, this concerns you, too, Nancy," Dad said, "so why don't you let us help you with the painting supplies, and then you can join our conversation."

"Okay," I said.

With the three of us carrying the additional supplies from my car, it only took a couple of minutes to get everything up to Prince Carlo's room. When we finished, we went back to the living room and Dad filled me in on what he and Prince Carlo had been talking about when I got there.

"I just talked to the FBI," Dad said. "Washington is beginning to feel the heat from some powerful politicians in Italy."

"They're friends of the members of my family who are against me," Prince Carlo said.

"They're pressing for Prince Carlo's extradition to Italy, so he can stand trial," Dad said. "The only thing that's keeping him here is the Italian ambassador in Washington, who, quite frankly, will probably lose his job over this if we lose."

"Are you serious?" I asked.

Prince Carlo nodded. "It's just as I told you, Nancy. These particular members of my family have been looking to write me out of the picture for years," he said. "Now they think they've found a way, and they're not about to give up."

"I'm at my wits' end legally, Nancy," Dad said. "I was wanting to know what your detective mind had been thinking about."

I couldn't possibly tell Dad and Prince Carlo that it had been hard to think about anything, with all the distractions. Only that morning I had finally admitted that one of the reasons I hadn't done more was because I hated to leave the house.

"I thought about talking to some of Mrs. Mahoney's relatives," I told them, "but I just haven't gotten around to doing it."

Dad seemed surprised. "That's really unlike you, Nancy," he said. "Is there something the matter?"

How could I admit that having to do Hannah's job and deal with the crowds outside our house were almost forcing me to be a hermit? I don't know if it was being worried about Hannah or the weirdness of having the press camping in my front yard, but this was ridiculous. Dad was right—this was not me!

"No, nothing," I replied. I looked at my watch. "In fact, if you two can manage without me for a couple of hours, I need to do some sleuthing."

"We wouldn't have it any other way," Dad said.

I went upstairs to my room, changed, then telephoned Mrs. Mahoney and told her that I needed to talk to her about the case. I was feeling like myself again.

"Come right over, Nancy," Mrs. Mahoney said. "I was just about to have tea, but I can wait on that, and then we can have it together."

The real Nancy Drew went downstairs, said good-bye to Dad and Prince Carlo, got in her car in the garage, and backed out onto the driveway. The real Nancy Drew just smiled at the people peering inside her car, looking for signs of Prince Carlo. The real Nancy Drew felt much, much better now that she had rejoined civilization. The real Nancy Drew made a promise that she would never lose track of herself again.

When I got to Mrs. Mahoney's mansion, I rolled down the driver's window, punched a button, told the voice on the intercom who I was, and right away the wrought-iron gates, each sporting a huge *M,* opened wide.

I drove up the winding road to the portico. Mrs. Mahoney's butler, whose name really is James, must have been waiting for me, because the front door opened before I had a chance to ring the bell. With a bow James said, "Come in, please, Ms. Drew. M'Lady is in the drawing room. Please come this way."

I mean, James actually talks this way. It's cool and weird at the same time. Outside of Mrs. Mahoney's house, you only hear this in the movies.

I joined Mrs. Mahoney in what Hannah would call the sitting room.

"Have a seat, dear, and let me pour you some tea," Mrs. Mahoney said.

"Thank you," I said.

"Sugar?" Mrs. Mahoney said.

"Two lumps, please," I told her.

Mrs. Mahoney spooned two sugar cubes into my cup and handed it to me.

I stirred it a couple of times and tasted it. "It's good," I told her.

"I have it blended especially for me in Sri Lanka," she said. "That used to be Ceylon, you know."

I nodded.

"Try some of these sandwiches here, Nancy," Mrs. Mahoney said. "Dora made them right before you came, and I'm sure they're lovely."

Mrs. Mahoney was right. I had never tasted such delicious crab salad in my life.

After a few more minutes of small talk, Mrs. Mahoney said, "Now, then, dear, what was it you wanted?"

"Do you have old letters or diaries or papers of

any sort that might shed light on Prince Carlo's situation?" I asked. "With Hannah in the hospital and with . . ." I stopped. I didn't need to make any excuses to Mrs. Mahoney. It was all totally irrelevant. "I thought that might be a good place to start."

I noticed Mrs. Mahoney blink at the word *start*. She probably thought I had almost solved the mystery by now.

"Well, you're in luck, dear," Mrs. Mahoney said, "because the Mahoneys never throw anything away." She stood up. "As a matter of fact, the attic of this house—and it's a huge attic, mind you—is full of trunks with letters from various relatives to members of both my family and my late husband's."

I suddenly gasped. Mrs. Mahoney gave me a puzzled look. It hadn't occurred to me to sort out whose family we were actually talking about here. Princess Teresa-Maria had said someone in Mrs. Mahoney's family had helped them during World War II, but we didn't know if that meant her family or her husband's family.

"When did you and Mr. Mahoney marry?" I asked her.

"Nineteen fifty," Mrs. Mahoney replied.

"So you weren't married during World War Two," I said. "That makes things interesting."

"I don't understand," Mrs. Mahoney said.

"Well, we've all been thinking that this relative Princess Teresa–Maria was talking about was *your* relative," I explained. "I'm not exactly sure how you fit into this picture, but maybe it was actually your *husband's* relative who helped the royal family."

"Well, that could be," Mrs. Mahoney said. "Cornelius had a brother, Julius, who lived with us for a while in his later years, and I think he served in World War Two. But he and Cornelius never cared much for each other, so I can't give you too much information about him."

I could easily understand that. Cornelius Mahoney, according to everything I had ever heard, was not a very nice man. In fact, some people in River Heights actually accused Mrs. Mahoney of giving away large sums of her money to try to make people forget just how awful Mr. Mahoney supposedly was. If his brother actually did help Prince Carlo's family, then it probably wouldn't have been something that Cornelius Mahoney would have admired, because he never liked to help people himself.

"Do you have any of Julius's letters or diaries in the attic?" I asked.

"Yes." Mrs. Mahoney let out a sigh. "Actually, Cornelius was against keeping Julius's things after he died, but I put my foot down. All of Julius's trunks are in the attic. Nothing has been touched."

"May I go through them?" I asked.

"Of course, dear," Mrs. Mahoney replied. "If you think this might help you solve the mystery."

I didn't know if it would or not, but things were beginning to look up.

7

Too Many Mysteries

Mrs. Mahoney personally took me up to her attic, which was as large as some people's houses.

"There's no dust up here," I remarked.

"Of course not!" Mrs. Mahoney arched an eyebrow. "There's no dust anywhere in my house, Nancy," she added, almost imperiously. "I have help to make sure it's always spotless."

That was probably a dumb thing for me to say, but frankly she was the first person I had ever met whose attic was dust free. I was glad, because if I was going to spend the next few days of my life going through Julius Mahoney's letters, papers, diaries—whatever I could find—then I didn't want to be sneezing constantly.

"I wish everyone felt that way," I told her sincerely. "Unfortunately I've ended up solving quite a few mysteries in dusty old attics."

"Well, maybe you won't have to do that, Nancy, if you can find the answer here," Mrs. Mahoney said. "Come this way."

I followed Mrs. Mahoney in between neatly stacked boxes and trunks, to a far corner of the attic. Although it wasn't as bright as it would have been in a normal room, there was still more light here than I had expected. There were also some comfortable-looking chairs spaced rather evenly throughout the attic, and I wondered if Mrs. Mahoney came up here often just to spend time remembering past events in her life. I didn't ask her because I thought that would be too personal. Anyway, that didn't have a whole lot to do with the mystery at hand.

"Here we are, Nancy," Mrs. Mahoney said. There was a dormer window nearby, and Mrs. Mahoney walked over and raised the shade. "Be sure and pull it back down when you've finished for the day," she added.

"Do all of these trunks belong to Julius?" I asked.

Mrs. Mahoney nodded. "I know there's a lot to go through, dear, but I think that Julius must have kept everything he ever owned." She sighed. "I don't know why I've kept it all, Nancy. It's just gathering dust." She looked up at me and grinned. "Figuratively speaking, of course!" she added with a chuckle. "Julius seemed so sad toward the end of his life. He had no one except Cornelius, and, well, I'm sure you've heard all the stories about my late husband. He wasn't as bad as people say he was, but he certainly wasn't as good as he could have been." She touched one of Julius's trunks. "Julius was a very good man. He was kind and gentle. I just couldn't throw out his things." Mrs. Mahoney turned and looked at me. "It would have been like admitting, well, that his life hadn't meant anything, and although we never talked about it, I just always thought it had."

"Well, I'm certainly going to see what I can discover, Mrs. Mahoney," I told her. I hoped I could find some connection that would not only corroborate Prince Carlo's story, but also prove that Julius Mahoney had achieved more in his life than his brother had believed. "Thank you again for letting me do this."

Mrs. Mahoney left, and I opened the first trunk. It was full of old clothes from several decades ago. The first thing I thought of was a story I had seen in the *Bugle* about the River Heights Little Theater Group asking people to donate any period clothes they could find for use in upcoming plays. These would be wonderful, but if Mrs. Mahoney had seen the article, I doubted she would have made the connection. I decided I'd mention that to her later because I couldn't think of a better use for these clothes. They'd be taken care of, I knew, and would only add to the authentic feel of the performances.

In the next trunk I found books, but not just any books. These were first editions. There were a lot of well-known novels, as well as some biographies and histories of different countries and cultures. What an addition these would make to the River Heights library. They shouldn't be stored in a trunk when they could do so much good elsewhere. I made a mental note to talk to Mrs. Mahoney about donating these books as well.

In the third trunk I hit pay dirt! It was full of letters and diaries, but I soon realized that everything had just been dumped into the trunk.

I decided to organize everything by date so that I could find the ones written during and after World War II. They would probably have the information I needed.

The first letters I sorted through predated the war, and I soon realized that Mrs. Mahoney had been right. Julius Mahoney had kept everything he had ever written or received! I felt like I was prying when I found love letters Julius had received from someone named Leticia Johnson. I also found letters he had written to her, which meant that Leticia had probably given them all back to him after their relationship ended. Since this didn't seem to have any connection to the mystery at hand, I put them all aside.

Near the bottom of the trunk, I found letters that Julius had written to his parents from college. It was weird to think that they were Mrs. Mahoney's in-laws. I scanned some of them, just to get a feel for his personality, and it was easy to see that what Mrs. Mahoney had observed was true: Julius was a kind, caring, and seemingly very gentle person. Most of the letters were about college life—and it was interesting to compare those times to what Ned told me about life at the university today. The last letter was dated December 7, 1941, the day Pearl Harbor was attacked. Julius had told his parents that he was going to enlist. There was nothing here that would help me solve the mystery of the Mahoney connection to Prince Carlo's family in Italy, but I was beginning to see a possibility, and I was hoping that I would find the evidence in another trunk.

I had to go through a couple more trunks of clothes and personal knickknacks, but I was soon rewarded. One of the bigger trunks contained all of Julius's letters and diaries written after he joined the army in early 1942. It was interesting to see the war censors at work. Some of what he had written had been cut out or blacked out, so it took a little extra effort to piece together exactly what was going on. He had probably been told what he could put in his letters and what he couldn't, because for the most part they were full of generalities—nothing that would head me in the right direction.

"Nancy?"

I turned, startled to find Mrs. Mahoney right behind me. "Yes?" I said.

"You father just called. He said your cell phone must be off," Mrs. Mahoney said. "They've moved Hannah to a regular room. She was asking for you."

I looked at my watch. I couldn't believe how much time had passed. "Thank you, Mrs. Mahoney."

"You go see her, then come back here," Mrs. Mahoney said, reading my mind. "In the meantime I'll have Dora fix us a snack, all right?"

"Oh, that would be great," I said. "I think I'm on to something here."

"I'm glad to hear that, dear." Mrs. Mahoney

glanced at trunks and boxes that contained Julius Mahoney's life. "He deserves that."

Mrs. Mahoney showed me to a bathroom, where I washed my hands and freshened up as best I could. Then I hurriedly left the house and headed for the hospital.

Dad was just coming out of Hannah's room when I got there.

"How is she?" I asked.

"Much better," Dad said.

"Great!" I said.

"How about you?" Dad asked. "Do you have anything good to report?"

"I'm getting there." I quickly told him about Julius Mahoney. "I just need a little more time to finish going through his things."

Dad nodded. "I need to get back home. Prince Carlo is all right, although I suppose I'm breaking the law by leaving him by himself. Technically he's not really by himself. Bess and George were cooking dinner when I left. They've really stepped up to the plate for us."

"They're the best," I told him. "See you later."

Hannah was sitting up when I went into her room.

"How are you feeling?" I asked her.

"I feel much better," Hannah replied. "The

doctors here seem to know what they're doing. I haven't felt this good in years."

"I am so glad to hear that, Hannah," I said. "We were worried about you."

"I didn't mean to alarm everyone." Hannah sniffed. "You're my family, and I need to be up, taking care of you."

"Don't you even think about it!" I said. "We've got everything under control."

Hannah sniffed again. "Well, I guess you probably could get along without me."

Well, that had been the wrong thing for me to say! "Hannah, you know how much we rely on you. I just didn't want you worrying," I said. "Dad just told me that Bess and George were cooking for Prince Carlo, so, well, you can only imagine what that's like."

"I definitely need to get well," Hannah said. "You tell them that I expect that kitchen to be in the same shape it was when I left it."

"I'll do that," I told her, glad that I was able to set things straight. "You just get better."

Hannah yawned. "I think I need to take another nap," she said.

I went over and kissed her on the forehead. "The rest will do you good," I told her. "I'm going back over to Mrs. Mahoney's. I think I'm close to finding a connection between Prince Carlo's family and Mr. Mahoney's."

But Hannah's snoring told me that she hadn't heard what I had just said, so I tiptoed out of the room and headed back to Mrs. Mahoney's.

What Mrs. Mahoney had ready for us to eat wasn't what I would personally consider a snack. To me a snack is a box of crackers I grab from the kitchen pantry at home, while Hannah protests that I'm going to ruin my appetite for the dinner she's been working on all day. Mrs. Mahoney's snack was something you might find as hors d'oeuvres in a really expensive restaurant.

"Wow!" I exclaimed. "This is great!"

"Dora's a superb cook," Mrs. Mahoney said. "While you're helping yourself, Nancy, tell me how Hannah is doing, and then, if you want to, fill me in on what you've found out so far."

"Okay." I picked up a plate, and while I was taking samples of almost everything, I told Mrs. Mahoney that Hannah was almost back to normal. "It won't be long before she's telling the hospital staff how to run the place, I'm sure."

"That's good," Mrs. Mahoney said. "Doctors expect that from older patients. When we start doing that, they know we're well, so they sign the papers to dismiss us."

I grinned. "As for Julius, here's where I am so far." I spent the rest of our snack time eating and bringing her up to date on what I had found out. "From what I've learned about him so far, I can easily believe that he would have helped Prince Carlo's family. He just seems to be that kind of a person."

"I agree, Nancy," Mrs. Mahoney said. "I most definitely agree."

Mrs. Mahoney insisted that I take a thermos and a basket of snacks with me up to the attic, so I did, thinking that this would allow me to work uninterrupted while I read through the letters from the war years. It didn't take many pages for a picture to emerge.

In 1944 Julius was in Italy, and in one particular letter he mentioned that he had met a wonderful family near Rome. He had secretly helped them recover their belongings from the Fascists in the Italian government and then hide them in a mountain chalet, but that was all he said. I read several letters beyond this particular one, and found nothing else about who this family was or what happened afterward. Were any of these letters missing? I wondered. Maybe Julius hadn't really known who he was helping? I could believe that he was the kind of person who wouldn't hesitate to help the poorest family in Rome—or the richest—if the people needed his help. It wouldn't matter to him. By the time I had finished reading the last letter in the trunk, the war was over, and Julius was headed home.

The last trunk contained no letters or diaries, only birthday cards from his parents. It occurred to me that nowhere had there been anything from Cornelius. I put everything back into the boxes and went back downstairs.

I found Mrs. Mahoney sitting alone in her library, reading a book and having a cup of tea.

"Won't you let me pour you some more tea, Nancy?" Mrs. Mahoney said.

"Please," I said. "I also have just a few questions, if you don't mind."

"I don't mind at all, dear." Mrs. Mahoney poured the tea, dropped in two lumps of sugar, stirred it, and then handed the cup to me. "What was it you wanted to know?"

"There were no letters after the war. It was almost as if Julius ceased to exist, although I know he didn't," I said. "What happened?"

Mrs. Mahoney took a sip of tea. "When Mr. Mahoney and I married, the war had been over for several years, and nobody really wanted to talk about it then," she said. "Julius was just finishing up his doctoral studies here at the university, so he was very busy—and very introverted, I thought. He didn't talk much to me—or to Cornelius, who was younger than Julius. At first I thought he was a bit conceited, but I soon realized that he was very unhappy about something, and I thought it might be something in his past, but, of course, I never found out. He lived with his parents until they died, and I know that was hard on him, especially his mother's death. He had his professorship here at the university, which is a little unusual because universities don't normally hire their own graduates, but Julius must have been very special. His students adored him and, from what I understand, he published articles in some of the most prestigious journals in his field."

"Really?" I said, interrupting her. "I'd love to see them."

"I'm sure you can find copies in the university library," Mrs. Mahoney said. "He left explicit instructions for everything in his office to be donated to the university library—his books, his professional manuscripts, things like that. He never seemed to mix his university life with his home life. He kept them separate."

"What did he teach at the university?" I asked.

"Italian—both the language and the literature," Mrs. Mahoney said. "Frankly the entire family was puzzled about that one. He had always been interested in math and science, and had originally planned to become an engineer. I guess the war changed him more than anybody ever thought."

Italian, I thought. Another piece of the puzzle fell into place. "If something happened to him while he was in Italy to make him change his mind, then whatever it was could be the connection we're looking for," I said.

"Good heavens, Nancy!" Mrs. Mahoney said. "Why didn't I see this myself?"

"What, the fact that Prince Carlo is from Italy and Julius taught Italian?" I said.

Mrs. Mahoney nodded.

"Well, I certainly think it might be the connection to Prince Carlo's family, but we need more evidence," I said. "Still . . ." I hesitated. "I did find something, but I don't want to get my hopes up." I showed her the letter Julius had written to his parents about helping a family recover their belongings from the Fascists and then hiding them in a mountain chalet.

"That must be it!" Mrs. Mahoney said. "It has to be the connection!"

"Do you mind if I make a copy of this letter?" I asked.

"Of course not!" Mrs. Mahoney said. "I want to help you any way I can!"

I didn't remember ever seeing Mrs. Mahoney so excited about anything before. It seemed like she would have been happier with Julius, even though she had been married to Cornelius Mahoney. Of course, I would never say that to her—and I doubted very seriously if she had ever admitted that to herself.

After I left Mrs. Mahoney's, I stopped by an office supply store and made a photocopy of the letter before I headed home. There were still a few people in front of our house when I pulled into the driveway.

Stepping out of my car in the garage, I could hear Bess and George laughing. I was glad they were trying to keep up Prince Carlo's spirits. I hoped what I had found out about Julius Mahoney would lift his spirits even more.

I found Bess, George, and Prince Carlo sitting in the living room, surrounded by stacks of letters.

"What in the world is going on?" I asked.

"Oh, this must be what it's like to be a famous movie star," George told me. "This bag of letters came today. They're all from teenage girls here in River Heights."

"Are you kidding me?" I said.

"No!" Bess said. "Listen to this one!"

Bess read the letter, which was a proposal of marriage.

"This girl has never even met him and yet she wants to marry him!" George said. "Is that crazy or what?"

"Hey!" Prince Carlo said. "It could happen."

We all laughed. I was glad that Prince Carlo seemed to be in a pretty good mood.

"Well, it may be crazy, but I think movie and TV stars get this all the time," I said.

Bess read a couple more letters, which were pretty funny, and then Prince Carlo said, "But the mail also brought something really nice."

"Oh, what?" I asked.

Prince Carlo stood up and went to the dining-room table. "I got some incredible sketches from someone," he said. "The person who did these is a true artist."

"I don't know a whole lot about art, but they sure do look familiar to me," Bess said. "I'm sure I've seen something like these in a museum."

"Or the person who sketched them could have

just copied them from some famous painting," George suggested.

"I don't think so," Prince Carlo said. "This is something I've never seen before. It's almost breathtaking in its originality."

"They're not signed?" I said.

Prince Carlo shook his head. "There was a note included, but it just said that the person wanted me to have these as a thank-you."

Bess giggled. "As a thank-you for thinking about the marriage proposal to come, probably," she said.

"Oh, you are such a cynic," I said.

"Well, you'll get that way if you read the rest of these letters, Nancy," George said.

"What about you, Nancy?" Prince Carlo said. "Did you find out anything that you think might help my case?"

I nodded and told them about Julius Mahoney's letter from Italy in 1944.

"That could be just what we're looking for!" Prince Carlo said. "This is wonderful!"

"Well, I don't want you to get your hopes up," I told him. "It could turn out to be some other family."

"That's true," he said with a grimace. "There were many families that needed help back then, and the

American soldiers were always there to come to their aid."

"How can you find out for sure?" Bess asked.

"I guess I could get on the telephone and start making some calls to the different members of Prince Carlo's family," I said. "I just hope they'll talk to me."

"How about trying the Internet," George suggested. "I can help you do the searches."

"I have a better idea. Why don't you fly to Italy? You can use my jet," Prince Carlo said. "Anyway, you'll probably have more luck if you talk to people in person."

8

Flight to Italy

Actually, I had been hoping that Prince Carlo would feel that way. It would make things easier. With all the technology available today, like e-mail and the Internet—not to mention the good old telephone—it really is possible to get a lot accomplished without traveling to a location. But I still believe that there's no substitute for talking face-to-face with someone who might be able to shed some light on the events surrounding a crime. Although Dad is very understanding about what I need to do—and the places I need to visit—in order to solve a mystery, I wasn't exactly sure how he'd react when I told him that I needed to go to Italy!

So when Dad got home from the office that

evening, I told him about the letter I had found from Julius Mahoney explaining how he helped an Italian family recover their belongings during World War II. "But I don't think I can finish solving this mystery without going to Italy this weekend, Dad."

I was all prepared to use Prince Carlo to support my argument, but Dad surprised me with, "Me either, Nancy."

For just a minute I was taken aback, but not for long. "Prince Carlo said we could use his jet. That should make it easier."

Dad nodded. "I checked with the FBI today about doing just that, because I thought they had impounded it for some reason. But I was told that there wouldn't be any problem."

"Nancy, Prince Carlo has been teaching me and George Italian," Bess said. "You could take us along as your interpreters."

"Parlo italiano molto bene!" George said.

"Great! I was planning to ask both of you to go, anyway," I told them, "but that's just another reason why you should." I turned to Dad. "Okay?"

"Of course," Dad said. "The more the merrier."

Uh-oh! I thought. There's a problem here. I looked at Prince Carlo. Dad must have been reading my thoughts.

"The United States Attorney's office has okayed the trip, Nancy, and there's no problem with Prince Carlo staying here," Dad said. "Hannah will be home from the hospital, although she's supposed to rest as much as possible, but knowing Hannah, 'as much as possible' won't be very much. Ned's agreed to stay here to help take care of things."

"When did you talk to Ned?" I said.

"This afternoon." Dad grinned. "You're not the only one who's been busy, Nancy. The rest of us have been too."

"Well, what are we waiting for, then?" I said. "We need to start packing."

"I think we need to eat first," Dad said. "I'm kind of hungry."

"Bess and I spent hours in the kitchen," George said. "Everything's all right. It just needs to be heated up some."

"You two are amazing," I told them. "I never knew you were so domestic!"

Bess giggled. "You don't have to be domestic to open up some cans, Nancy!"

"You're not giving yourselves enough credit, girls," Prince Carlo said. "I'm sure I've already gained several pounds because of your gourmet cooking."

"Well, it all sounds good to me," Dad said. "Let's eat."

Just as we started into the dining room, the door-bell rang. "I wonder who that could be," I said as I headed for the front door. It was Ned.

"Ned! We were just talking about you!" I told him. I stood aside to let him come in. "You're just in time for dinner, too."

"I'll sit with you and have a soda or something, but I had a late lunch, so I'm really not hungry." Ned handed me a cardboard tube. "This was on the front porch. I just wanted to come by to see if you discovered anything important from talking to Mrs. Mahoney."

I looked at the cardboard tube. It was addressed to Prince Carlo. "Well, not from talking to her," I told him, as we headed for the dining room, "but I did find an important piece of the puzzle."

Bess and George were presiding over a buffet of sorts.

"Prince Carlo, you have a package," I said, handing him the tube. "They must not have rung the bell when they delivered it. That happens sometimes."

"I wonder what it is." Prince Carlo lifted off the plastic end and peered inside. "Oh! I think I know." He looked at us. "Did you see who delivered this?"

"No, it was already on the porch when I got here," Ned said, as we got in the buffet line behind Dad.

"This looks really great," he added. "Maybe I will have something to eat after all."

I told Ned that I thought it was wonderful that he had agreed to stay with Prince Carlo and Hannah while we went to Italy, but I didn't mention that I had been secretly hoping that he could go with us.

"It's no problem at all, Nancy. I'm glad to help out," Ned said as he spooned himself servings of every dish Bess and George had set out. "I have two major English projects due at the beginning of next week, and your house will be a great place to get them done."

"Really?" I said.

Ned nodded. "When I'm at the university library, people keep interrupting me to help them with their projects, and while I usually don't mind, I get behind on my own work, and I need to concentrate on what I'm doing," he said. "Mom and Dad are having some friends in from Washington DC this weekend, and I think they've invited half of River Heights for a couple of receptions."

"I was right!" Prince Carlo had taken the contents out of the tube and was holding them up for us to see. "These are some more sketches by the mystery artist."

"Oh, those are nice!" Dad said. "What 'mystery' artist?"

"Some more were delivered earlier," Bess said.

"They were mailed," George added. "The postman delivered them."

Prince Carlo looked at the tube. "No postage. No address. Just my name in black felt-tip pen." He looked up at everyone. "The artist obviously delivered these sketches in person." He sighed. "I'd love to talk to whoever drew these. I have some questions about the technique. It's amazing."

"Who in the world in River Heights would be sending sketches?" Bess asked. She paused for a moment, thinking, then blurted out, "Do you think they're behind some of your problems, Prince Carlo?"

"I don't think so," Prince Carlo said. "I'd probably be getting threatening letters, instead of these wonderful drawings."

"That's right." Bess looked at me and grinned. "No wonder I'm not the detective in the group."

"It is odd, though," I told her. "I wonder why she didn't sign them."

"Why 'she'?" Dad said.

"The style," I replied. "I think it belongs more to a woman than to a man."

"That's not concrete, of course, but intuition does

play a big role in detection," Dad said. He looked at everyone else. "Especially *Nancy's* intuition."

Dad was right. I often have to rely on my intuition, when I'm not having much luck finding concrete evidence. But once I follow what I think is the right path, I always succeed in finding the evidence that will stand up in court.

Prince Carlo gave us his interpretation of the sketches, complete with where he thought the artist had studied. "I see an incredible mixture of styles," he said. "Whoever did this has such an excellent sense of adaptation. Take a look at these lines, for instance. They remind me of Lubrano in Rome, but he takes so few students, that . . . well, his work is the only other place I've seen this. And look here," he added, pointing to the top of one of the sketches. "This is Cortina in Florence. There is no other artist who knows how to do this, so this can only be someone who studied with him."

Prince Carlo continued pointing out various things about the sketches that, he repeated, showed not only the influence of some of the best painters in Italy, but also an individuality in how the styles were rendered on paper.

"Absolutely amazing," he said. "Absolutely amazing. It's too bad I don't have a view of the front of your house," he added. "I could sit and wait for the artist to deliver the next set of sketches."

"Do you think that'll happen?" George asked.

"Of course it'll happen," Bess said. "There's more to this than just art."

Prince Carlo blushed. "I guess we can always hope," he said with a grin.

Bess and George and I agreed to clean up the kitchen, so Dad and Prince Carlo could discuss what Dad needed to do in Italy and Ned could find out exactly what he was expected to do while he was staying at our house. Just then the telephone rang.

"Hello," I said. "Hannah! Are you all right?"

That wasn't a very bright question, I know, because Hannah launched right into how, if she hadn't been all right, she wouldn't be calling me, and that she had told the hospital that she was well enough to go home and that she wanted to go home right then.

"I made them call my doctor, so he would come to the hospital and sign the release forms," Hannah told me. "They didn't want to do it because he was at some fancy party, but I wasn't going to take no for an answer."

"Well, we'll be right there to pick you up," I told her.

"I've already called a cab, and it should be here any minute," Hannah said, "so you just keep on doing what you're doing, and I'll see you in a few minutes."

Before I could protest, I heard Hannah shouting something, then there was a click.

I told everyone what she had done.

"Get the name of that medicine," Bess said. "I want to make sure that's what I take if I ever get sick. This has been a miraculous recovery."

"I guess," I said. "I'm not sure." Hannah seemed more than back to her old self. I hope she leveled off some before she got home. I looked at Ned. "I'm not quite sure your staying here is such a wonderful idea after all," I told him.

"Why not?" Ned asked.

"Hannah can be really possessive of this house, that's why," I said. "You might feel useless."

"I wouldn't worry about Ned," Dad interjected. "I have a feeling that Hannah still needs some taking care of, and I think she'll be glad that Ned is here so she can rest from time to time."

Dad's insight is amazing sometimes. When we heard the taxi pull up in the drive, I braced myself for a possible storm, but when Hannah came in, the first thing she said was, "Ned, dear, would you mind getting my suitcase for me? I'm a bit winded."

"I wouldn't mind at all, Hannah," Ned said. He winked at me. "I'll be right back."

Hannah sat down at the kitchen table and let us fuss over her for a while. From time to time I saw her looking around, probably trying to see just what was out of place, but when she didn't say anything, I figured she wasn't bothered by what she saw. Bess and George had done a good job keeping Hannah's kitchen in order.

Dad also told Hannah about the upcoming trip to Italy and that Ned would be staying in the house to help her with whatever she needed.

"Oh, that's wonderful news," Hannah said. "I guess I don't have as much strength as I thought I did."

"You probably just used it all up between here and the hospital," I told her. "You'll get it back by morning, and you'll just keep getting stronger."

"Well, I think I'd better lie down," Hannah finally said. "I'm feeling a little droopy right now."

I went with Hannah to her room, which is just off the kitchen, but down a little hallway, and actually quite private. I turned down the covers of her bed while she finished in her bathroom. Then, just like she did for me, for many, many years, I tucked her in, and I turned out the light.

"Good night, Nancy," Hannah whispered. "Thank

you so much. You're so wonderful to me."

"Good night, Hannah," I whispered back. "I'm so glad you're home. We missed you. We really did."

"I know, dear," Hannah said. "I know."

The next morning Ned arrived early with a couple of suitcases, one with his clothes and toiletries and the other with his books. I helped him carry everything up to the guest bedroom next to Prince Carlo's.

I had just finished helping Ned unpack, when Bess and George arrived with their bags. I needed to put a couple more things into my suitcase, and then I would be ready to leave. Dad's bags were already in his car.

Just as I started out of Ned's room, he whispered, "Nancy!"

I turned. He had a funny look on his face. "What's wrong?" I asked.

"You don't think this is a setup, do you?" Ned asked.

"A *setup*?" I said.

Ned nodded. "Prince Carlo seems like an all-right guy, but some of the most notorious criminals in history have been very likeable," he said.

I went back into the room. "Where's this coming from?" I asked.

"Our visitors," Ned replied.

"You mean the people visiting your parents from Washington?" I said.

"Yes. It seems that Prince Carlo and his troubles are the talk of Washington."

"Why?" I asked.

Ned shrugged. "I didn't want to look like I was eavesdropping, so I only got what I could hanging around the buffet table when I got home last night."

"Are you saying that you think Prince Carlo might try to escape while we're gone?" I said.

"I don't know," Ned said. "I just thought I should tell you what I had heard."

"Well, he certainly has his detractors, Ned," I told him. "Maybe your parents' friends are just repeating rumors they've heard."

"That could be," Ned said.

"I think there are people who want others to think Prince Carlo would do something like that," I told Ned, "but I guess it wouldn't hurt to be extra careful."

This time, just as I left the room, Prince Carlo was coming out of his. He still looked sleepy. I was hoping he hadn't overheard the conversation I'd had with Ned.

"We're about to leave," I told him. "I'm glad you're

up, so we can say good-bye. Any last minute instructions?"

"Yes." He gave me a wry smile. "Don't believe everything you hear."

I swallowed hard. Now I really wondered if he had heard Ned and me talking. "I won't," I assured him. "I always keep an open mind."

Ned came out of the bedroom, acting as if we had never had our conversation. "Good morning," he said to Prince Carlo.

"Good morning," Prince Carlo replied.

It was a friendly greeting, and I couldn't read anything else into it.

"I hope you get a lot of work done while you're here," Prince Carlo added. "I promise I won't be any trouble."

Uh-oh! I thought. I spoke too soon.

Ned smiled. "I wasn't worried," he said. "I make my own decisions about people."

With that, we headed downstairs. Dad, Bess, and George were waiting for us.

"I'm going to say good-bye to Hannah," I said.

When I got to her room, she was just waking up. I kissed her forehead, told her to let Ned fix breakfast for her, but she pooh-poohed that idea, and said she was tired of being waited on.

Ned and Prince Carlo waved to us as we headed down the street toward the River Heights Regional Airport. We only had to plow through a few paparazzi. It seemed early morning was the time to fly with royalty.

"Do you think everything will be all right, Dad?" I asked when he turned a corner.

He looked over at me. "Yes," he said. "Are you worried about anything?"

I didn't answer right away. Finally I said, "Not really."

I had to trust my instincts. Despite the Washington gossip Ned had passed along, I honestly felt that Prince Carlo was innocent and could be trusted while we were gone.

"Good," Dad said.

"This is going to be one fabulous trip, I think," Bess said.

"Definitely," George agreed. "I wonder if the pilot will let me fly the plane for a little while."

I looked back at her. "You're kidding, right?"

George gave me a puzzled look. "Why would I be kidding?"

"I can answer that," Bess said. "If you're not kidding, then Mr. Drew, would you please drop me off at my house?"

"Okay, okay, I'm kidding," George said.

As we turned into the airport entrance, I saw Prince Carlo's gleaming jet parked at Gate 1, at the far end of the terminal. I felt chills go up and down my whole body. In just a few minutes we'd all be inside that plane, headed for Italy, and, I hoped, the final solution to the mystery.

9

Princess Teresa-Maria's Palace

You need to fasten your seat belts," the pilot's voice said over the intercom, awakening me. "We're about to land in Milano." He used the Italian name for a city I knew better as Milan.

I let out a sigh of relief, not only because the long trip was almost over, but because I had been dreaming about one of my previous cases. Actually, it had been more of a nightmare than a dream. In this one everything that had been right in real life had turned wrong, and I was being chased all over River Heights by people yelling, "You're a fake! You're a fake!"

I looked across the aisle at Bess and George, who were still asleep. They could both sleep through an earthquake. Dad was in Prince Carlo's private cabin at the rear of the plane. We had seen it just before we took off. It looked like a suite at a five-star hotel. Dad had actually offered it to one of us, but we all three decided he'd get more rest and have more privacy if he stayed there.

Out the window I could see land, and I thought about the couple of weeks I had spent in Milan two years ago with Ned and his family. Mr. Nickerson was interviewing a former Italian prime minister for a magazine article he was writing. It had been one of the best vacations I'd ever had. Milan is a very sophisticated city, and we were treated to meals in the best restaurants as well as VIP tours of the city. I doubted if this trip would be anywhere as nice as that one. The people we planned to see probably wouldn't be so welcoming.

I looked at my watch. It was still on River Heights time, so I calculated the difference and changed it. I thought about calling Ned, just to see how things were, but I didn't want to awaken him. Ned is one of those people who can't go back to sleep after they're disturbed. I'd call him later to find out how things were going.

Just then George let out a loud yawn. "I was dreaming all about Italian food," she said. "I can hardly wait to make that dream come true."

Bess stood up. "I'm still amazed that this plane has four bathrooms," she said. "I'm going to freshen up before we land. Milan is the fashion capital of Italy, and I don't want to look as though I buy all my clothes at a secondhand store."

"There's nothing wrong with that," George said. "You won't believe some of the bargains I got last week at that place across from the—"

"This is your pilot again. The noise you hear will be the wheels lowering," he said. "Please make sure your seat belts are fastened for landing at the Monza Airfield."

"I thought we were landing at Milan," Bess said, sitting back down and rebuckling her safety belt. She turned to me. "What happened to Milan?"

"Monza is a town just outside there," I told her. "It's closer to where Prince Carlo's family lives."

Actually, I had made a point of getting my bearings on the Net right before I went to sleep the night before, and I had brought along a small guide to the northern part of Italy. Although Monza was now more or less a suburb of Milan, at one time it was one of the most important cities in Lombardy, the region we'd be spending most of our time in. Theodolinda, the sixth-century Lombard queen, had Monza's first cathedral built, and then bequeathed all her wealth to the town. Prince Carlo traced his lineage to this royal family.

The pilot made a smooth landing and started taxiing toward a small hangar. There wasn't much to this airport from what I could see, but I guessed it suited Prince Carlo to keep his jet here. Then the pilot made a sharp turn, and I saw a larger building, which was surrounded by other private jets, and I suddenly changed my mind. This was obviously where very rich people kept their toys. There was no telling how many millions of dollars—or I should say euros—had been spent to buy these jets.

Finally the pilot parked the plane at one of the gates, and the ground crew began maneuvering the ramp toward the door.

The cockpit door opened, and one of the pilots came out, stretched, and said, "*Buongiorno, signorine!* Welcome to Italy!"

"*Grazie!*" we all said in unison.

"You did a great job flying this thing," George said. "I was going to ask you if you'd show me how the computers work, but I fell asleep instead. Maybe on the way back."

The pilot smiled. "No problem," he said. "We're actually early, so the car to your hotel isn't here yet. You still have time to freshen up if you'd like."

"Definitely!" Bess unbuckled her seat belt and headed toward "her" bathroom.

George and I did the same. On the way, I knocked on Dad's door.

"Come in," he called.

I opened the door slightly. *"Buongiorno,"* I said.

Dad smiled. *"Buongiorno."* He stood up and stretched. "I can't believe we're here already."

"You didn't get any sleep, did you?" I said.

Dad shook his head. "I never could sleep on a plane, even one as comfortable as this. Anyway, I was writing down some questions I want to ask various people in and around Milan." He sighed. "Nancy, this may seem clear-cut, but a lot of people have a lot riding on it, so we need to be careful."

"What do you mean, Dad?" I asked.

"I had a long, heart-to-heart talk with Prince Carlo right before we left," Dad said, "and he finally admitted that there are some very unsavory members in his family, and they aren't above hurting people to get what they want."

That doesn't sound good, I thought. "We'll be careful," I told him. "I promise."

"I know you will," Dad said, "but it helps to hear it again."

"Well, I need to get ready to work," I said. "It shouldn't take long."

I was actually amazed that fifteen minutes later we were all standing at the cabin door, carry-on bags in hand, ready to go into the terminal.

"Your driver, Franco, will meet you at the gate," the pilot said. "He'll take you to your hotel and be available to drive you wherever you need to go while you're in Italy."

"I hope he's in one of those really fast Italian cars," Bess whispered to me as we started down the ramp toward the gate.

George grinned. "That way we could see the sights in style."

"We're just here for a long weekend," I said. "I don't think there will be too much time for sightseeing. Anyway," I reminded them, "we're here to solve a mystery, and I'm going to need your help."

"I was only talking about 'after hours,' Nancy," Bess said. "You don't expect us to work twenty-four hours a day, do you?" She giggled, letting me know that she was just kidding.

Actually, I didn't know what to expect. "Let's just play it by ear," I said.

When we came to the gate area, there was a gorgeous and muscular hunk holding a sign that said: NANCY DREW.

Bess stopped. "Oh, my!"

"You can say that again," whispered George.

"What's wrong, girls?" Dad said behind us.

He looked over my shoulder. "Oh, I see the reason for the holdup. Well, let's not keep Franco waiting," he said with a grin.

I walked up to Franco, extending my hand. "I'm Nancy Drew."

"Welcome to Italy," Franco said with a big smile.

I introduced everyone, and they all shook hands, with Bess's handshake lingering just a little longer than it probably should have, but I figured that Franco was probably used to that.

"Your other luggage is already in the automobile," Franco said. "There's room enough in the trunk for your carry-ons, too."

Since this was a private airport, Franco was able to park right outside the gate, so we didn't have far to walk. I could tell that Bess was disappointed when she saw that we'd be going to our hotel in a really powerful-looking Mercedes instead of a Ferrari or some other Italian sports car, but I wasn't sure where she thought we'd all sit or put our luggage. Still, when we were all inside, buckled in, Franco left the airport as though he was racing at the Autodromo Nazionale, which I knew was in a large park just at the edge of Monza.

"Do you have the address of our hotel in Milan?" Dad asked Franco.

"*Si,* Signor Drew," Franco replied, "but Giovanna has requested that you come immediately to stay at Princess Teresa-Maria's house in Cernobbio."

We all looked at one another. This was a change of plans we hadn't expected.

"Are you sure that's all right?" I said. "We certainly don't want to impose."

"Oh, it's quite all right," Franco said. "Giovanna insisted, and Giovanna usually gets what Giovanna wants."

I looked over at Dad, who didn't seem concerned, so I just leaned back and let myself enjoy the passing countryside.

"What kind of a town is Cernobbio?" George asked.

"It's a resort town on Lake Como," Franco said. "Have you ever heard of Lake Como? It's very beautiful."

"I've seen pictures of it on the Internet," George said.

"Cernobbio was a favorite resort of Queen Caroline of England," Franco explained. "She stayed there during her exile. In fact, Princess Teresa-Maria owns an estate where Queen Caroline once lived."

"Are you talking about the Villa d'Este?" I asked, remembering my history.

"Oh, no, that's a hotel now," Franco said, "but Princess Teresa-Maria's estate isn't far from there."

Soon we were in sight of the mountains and rugged hillsides that surround Lake Como, which is a long, narrow lake in the shape of a wishbone. When we reached the town of Como, Franco stopped at Metropole and Suisse au Lac, a hotel with a terrace restaurant that he said had wonderful food and a magnificent view of the lake.

Franco was right about both. It took us twice as long to eat lunch because we kept getting distracted by all the activity on the lake. We watched as very wealthy people docked their yachts at the restaurant pier and passed us on their way to wherever they were going.

We each ordered something different from the menu, so we could share.

I had *costolette alla milanese*—wonderful veal cutlets. George had *manzo brasato al Barolo*—incredible lean beef. Bess had *spezzatino di pollo*—delicious chicken. Dad had *risotto alla milanese*—a tasty rice dish. And Franco had a pizza. We couldn't believe it, and we kidded him about it all during the meal. But we still ate the pieces he put on our plates, and it certainly tasted a hundred times better than any of the pizza I had ever eaten in River Heights. There are several places in town where Ned and I go that have really good Italian food. I hoped that this experience wouldn't ruin them for me. I certainly couldn't afford to fly to Italy every weekend just for lunch!

Franco didn't seem in any particular hurry, but it wasn't long until our American tendency to rush kicked in, and the four of us started getting our things together so we could get on with the day. After all, we weren't going to be in Italy that long, and we needed to accomplish as much as we could during that time. I'm sure Prince Carlo wouldn't be too happy if I told him that I wasn't able to solve the mystery because I spent too much time eating!

When we left the restaurant, Bess, George, and I leaned back in the plush leather seats of the Mercedes and closed our eyes as we rounded the southwest corner of the lake and headed toward Cernobbia. I knew I'd miss some really great scenery, but jet lag was suddenly catching up with us, and we needed to be rested as much as possible for the work ahead.

I hadn't meant to fall asleep, but when I next opened my eyes, Franco was waiting for the iron gates to open so we could drive up to Princess Teresa-Maria's estate.

"Wow!" George said sleepily. "I feel like I'm in an Italian fairy tale."

"Me too," Bess agreed.

I could see Princess Teresa-Maria's estate through a stand of tall pines. Like many of the Italian villas pictured in my guidebook, it had two uneven bell towers. I wondered what it would be like to be one of her grandchildren, to visit her here and be allowed to explore all the nooks and crannies of such a place. I was sure there were all kinds of mysteries associated with this palace. Maybe that's what Giovanna had in mind—letting us look for anything that would clear her beloved Prince Carlo's name.

Franco pulled up at the front entrance to the palace just as a tall woman with iron gray hair opened a door and stepped out. She had a stern look on her face.

"That's Giovanna," Franco said.

"She looks scary!" Bess said.

"She's really not," Franco said. "I think she's just worried about Prince Carlo. We all are."

Franco hopped out and opened the doors for us. Giovanna shook hands with all of us. "Welcome," she said.

Behind her an elderly man and a woman appeared.

"Canova and Carlotta will take your luggage to your rooms. I have coffee and dessert for you in the kitchen." She looked at us. "If that's all right. With the princess in the hospital, that's mostly where I've been eating."

"That's fine, Giovanna," I said. "We're easy house guests."

"Nancy's right, Giovanna," Dad said. "We're here on business, so we don't expect any special treatment."

I noticed that Giovanna's eyes relaxed slightly. I could tell she was so distracted by what had happened to both Princess Teresa-Maria and Prince Carlo that she would find it difficult to cope with demanding house guests.

The coffee and the cake were delicious, but I was glad when I felt we could excuse ourselves, so Bess, George, and I could get started. I wanted to look through Princess Teresa-Maria's letters and diaries. I had the feeling that's where I would find the answer I was looking for.

"I've arranged to meet with some of the members of the family and their lawyers in Milan," Dad told Franco. "As I understand it, you're available to drive me wherever I need to go." He removed a piece of paper from his coat pocket and handed it to Franco.

"Here's a schedule of the appointments I've made so far. It's not everybody, but it's a start."

"I think I can add to this list," Franco told Dad.

"Good." Dad looked at me. "Good luck with your search."

Prince Carlo had told me that his great-grandmother had never let anyone read her letters and diaries, but he hoped they might contain information about our mystery. After Dad and Franco left, Giovanna said, "There are many trunks belonging to Princess Teresa-Maria stored in the main bell tower, so that's where I think you should look. I think there are letters and diaries in there."

"Why won't she let anyone see them?" I asked.

"What's unusual about that?" Giovanna said. "They're very personal."

"I wonder if she would feel differently and let people look at them if she knew that Prince Carlo was in trouble," Bess said.

Giovanna shrugged. "She's not herself these days. I think she's had a series of small strokes which have affected her thinking," she said. "It would be hard to say. If she were thinking right, then of course she would, but she's not thinking right, so there's no telling. I'm just thankful that you're willing to help."

As we reached the final set of stairs leading up to the bell tower, Carlotta stepped out from behind a corner, startling us all and blocking our way.

"Where are you going?" Carlotta demanded in Italian.

I was taken aback by her threatening tone. So were Bess and George. We all looked at Giovanna to see what she would do.

"This is none of your concern, Carlotta," Giovanna said. "You need to stay out of it."

Instead of stepping aside, though, Carlotta said, "Princess Teresa-Maria's things are not to be touched. She has given strict orders, and you know that."

Even in the dim light, I could see Giovanna's face turning angry. She turned to us. "Follow me," she said.

At first I thought Carlotta was physically going to force us back down the stairs, but instead she started down herself, saying, "Prince Paolo will be angry when he discovers what you're doing."

I heard an intake of breath from Giovanna, but she didn't say anything until we had reached the next landing. "She is an evil woman, that Carlotta," she whispered, "but Princess Teresa-Maria would never listen to me when I told her she couldn't be trusted."

"Who's Prince Paolo?" I asked.

"Princess Teresa–Maria's son, and Prince Carlo's grandfather," Giovanna said. "He's worthless. He's gone through several fortunes. He's the reason Princess Teresa–Maria wants Prince Carlo to head the family."

"I guess that Carlotta is going to let him know what we're up to," I said.

Giovanna nodded. "When he finds out, he'll try to stop you, if he thinks that you'll find any information," she said.

"I'm hoping that I find something," I said.

"Where's Prince Carlo's father?" Bess asked. "Wouldn't he be the next one in line?"

"He was killed in a skiing accident when Prince Carlo was just a baby," Giovanna said. "If he were alive, then, well . . ."

We had reached a door at the top of a landing, and her voice drifted off. She took a large key out of her pocket, inserted it into the lock, and opened the door. Although it wasn't as clean as Mrs. Mahoney's attic, it didn't have as much dust as I had expected.

"I don't know how much time you have now," Giovanna said.

"We'll work fast," I said. I took a look at the huge

tower room that was completely filled with boxes, trunks, and chests of various kinds. "I promised Prince Carlo we'd solve this mystery, and that's what we're going to do!"

10

The Secret in the Old Attic

Giovanna **left us and** headed back downstairs.

"She may not be able to stop Prince Paolo from coming up here," I told Bess and George, "but I think she can intimidate him long enough so that maybe we can find *something* that will help us solve this mystery."

I was trying to sound positive, but I was somewhat overwhelmed too. The room was almost full, and boxes and trunks were stacked on top of one another almost to the ceiling.

Bess was shaking her head. "Where do we start?" she asked forlornly. "It could take us months to look through all of this."

"We don't have months," I said.

"That's the problem," George agreed.

"Well, we're not getting anywhere talking about it," I said. "Let's start opening trunks."

When Bess started to open the trunk closest to the door, I stopped her. "If Princess Teresa-Maria is like most people, she probably puts the most recent things to store on the outside," I said, "which means that the older things will be closer to the far wall."

"That makes sense," George said. "Let's start there."

As we started weaving our way through the room, Bess stopped at one of the windows. Even though it was covered with a dusty film, it still had a magnificent view of Lake Como.

"It's too bad we can't just sit here and enjoy the scenery," Bess said with a sigh.

"I know," I told her. "Maybe later."

When we finally reached the far wall, I managed to grab hold of the handle of a suitcase by standing on tiptoes, and I pulled it from the top of a pile of boxes and cases. It was heavier than I expected, and halfway down it slipped out of my hands, landing with a thud and sending up a cloud of dust.

Bess and George sneezed.

The fasteners were rusted, so it took me a few

minutes working with them to get the suitcase open, but there were only clothes inside. I let out a sigh of disappointment.

"This won't help," I said.

"Oh, those are such gorgeous dresses!" Bess squatted down and started lifting some of them out.

"Bess, we don't have time for a fashion show," I told her. "We have to—"

"Oh, look at this, Nancy!" Bess said, interrupting me, her voice full of excitement. "I think we're in the right place."

George and I crowded around her.

"What do you mean?" I asked.

Bess held up a piece of paper. "I think it's a sales receipt." She studied the yellowed sheet. "It's from a shop in Milan, and it's dated March twelfth, 1944."

I took it from her. "Fantastic!" I stood up and looked around. "Let's get to work."

For the next several minutes the three of us opened as many trunks and boxes as we could. Most of them contained clothes, but some of them had pictures and other personal items. Unfortunately there were no letters or diaries or other papers.

"What if Princess Teresa-Maria didn't save her letters or didn't write in a diary?" Bess said. "I don't."

I stood up. Bess had just put into words what I hadn't wanted to think about. Not everyone does things like that. I had to admit that I don't save every letter I receive, and except for my case notes I haven't written in a diary since my first couple of years of high school.

I was just about to admit defeat when George shouted, "I found them!"

Naturally the trunk was on the bottom of a stack, so it had taken us almost an hour to get to it, but it was full of letters and papers, so I was hoping that this really was what we were looking for.

"Set aside anything before—" I stopped. "Did you hear something?"

Bess and George listened.

"It sounds like shouting," George said.

"I wonder if Prince Paolo has arrived to try to stop us," Bess said.

I needed to gain us some time. Suddenly I had an idea. I remembered that Giovanna had left the key in the lock on the outside of the door. I weaved my way back through the room, took the key out of the lock, shut the door and locked it from the inside. It worked.

"Bess, George!" I called. "I need a pen and some paper fast. Bring me my notebook."

George was there in seconds, with Bess following close behind. "What's the plan?" she asked.

"You'll see," I told her.

I quickly wrote out: *Giovanna, We found what we were looking for. We've gone back to Milan. Nancy*

I unlocked the door, pushed a corner of the note under the end of the ornate metal plate that covered the lock, then George and I went back inside the room, and I locked the door from the inside again.

"We have to be very quiet, or this won't work," I whispered to them, "but I'm hoping that when Prince Paolo finally forces his way up here—with Giovanna berating him all the way up the stairs, I'm sure—they'll find the note and think that we're gone."

"What if there's another key?" George whispered.

"I doubt if there is, it's such an old lock, but we'll just hope there isn't," I told her.

"What if he breaks the door down?" Bess said.

"I don't think he'd do that," I said. "Frankly, I think when he reads that we've gone to Milan, he'll come after us."

The noise outside the door was getting louder, and the three of us knew that Prince Paolo and Giovanna were headed up the stairs, so we hurried back to the open trunk to try to find something that would clear Prince Carlo's name.

Within minutes I heard Giovanna shouting in Italian, and I recognized the words *Principe Paolo,* so I knew our "enemy" had arrived. When they reached the door, Giovanna found the note and read it aloud in English. That was followed by some angry Italian from Prince Paolo.

The three of us kept reading, hoping that our ruse would work. At first I was sure it hadn't, because Prince Paolo started pounding on the door, but almost as quickly, we heard a noise that sounded like someone running back down the stairs, and then all was quiet. I didn't know if Giovanna actually believed the note, but I didn't plan to leave the room until I had found what we were looking for.

Two hours later, we did.

I was skimming through Princess Teresa-Maria's diary from 1944 when I found an entry that mentioned a letter her husband, Prince Enzo, had written to thank the man who had helped them recover their belongings from the Fascists and then hide everything in their mountain chalet. The only problem was that, according to the diary, Prince Enzo hid the letter in the chalet!

"Why would he do something like that?" Bess asked.

"What?" I said. "Write the letter or hide it?"

"Both!" George said.

"That's what we need to find out," I said. "I wonder if Giovanna knows where this mountain chalet is. And I wonder if the letter is even still there—if it's true that it was there in the first place. I'd say it's worth an investigation."

"Well, we can't stay here forever," George said. "We need to go ask her."

"What if Prince Paolo is still downstairs?" Bess said.

"We'll just have to take a chance. We have to search that mountain chalet," I said. "Franco said he was at our disposal. If Giovanna knows where it is, and it's reachable, I'll call Franco on his cell phone and see if he can drive us there."

We quickly—and quietly—arranged the trunks the way they were when we found them. After we finished, I decided that only a superdetective would be able to tell where we had been looking.

I unlocked the door, opened it slowly, and looked out. Nobody was hiding behind it, ready to jump us.

The three of us slipped out onto the landing. I

relocked the door, and we started downstairs. As old as they were, the steps leading down from the bell tower were remarkably sturdy and didn't creak at all.

We were on the second floor when we encountered Carlotta, who looked as though she had seen a ghost.

"You are gone!" Carlotta said. "You are gone!"

"We are now," I told her with a smile.

She just stared at us, as we continued on down to the first floor, where I hoped we'd find Giovanna. She was sitting at the kitchen table, a cup of coffee in front of her, looking forlorn. But when she glanced up and saw us, she got the biggest smile on her face that I had ever seen.

"I thought you might still be in the room, I really did, but I couldn't be sure, and I didn't want to take a chance on exposing your secret." She stood up. "It's true what I read about you, Nancy Drew! It really is!"

When I gave Giovanna a puzzled look, she said, "Oh, I may be an old lady, but I know how to use the Internet, and I've read all about you these last few days." She laughed. "Prince Paolo was so angry. He really thought you had already left the palace, so he telephoned a friend of his with the Milan police, and he's racing there at this very moment to try to find you and to get back whatever it was you 'stole.'"

"Actually, we didn't 'steal' anything," I said, "but we did find the next clue."

"We need to go to the mountain chalet," George said. "Do you know where it is?"

Giovanna gasped. "Of course, but why do you need to go there? None of the family has used it in years, and I'm sure it's in disrepair."

I told Giovanna what Princess Teresa-Maria had written in her diary, and she said, "That sounds so unlike Prince Enzo. He was such a greedy, uncaring man." She shook her head in dismay. "Prince Paolo is just like his father."

"I have a feeling that letter is still there, and I believe that it will mention Julius Mahoney by name," I told Giovanna. "If we can find it, then it will prove that Prince Carlo was not making up the story about why Princess Teresa-Maria wanted to give that painting to Mrs. Mahoney."

Carlotta appeared suddenly at the doorway and just stood there staring at us.

With a fierceness I had not seen from her before, Giovanna flew at her, shaking her fist. Carlotta took off running, and I thought for a minute that Giovanna would follow, but she remained where she was. Finally she turned around and said, "She'll find a way to contact Prince Paolo, I know, and he'll come back here. You have to get to the chalet and look for that letter without Prince Paolo knowing what you're doing."

That sounded ominous. I couldn't imagine having to face Prince Paolo high in the Italian Alps. He struck me as being a person who wouldn't think twice before he threw someone off a cliff, if it suited his purpose.

"We thought we could get Franco to take us," I told Giovanna. "Do you think he would?"

"Yes. Franco knows the mountains," Giovanna said, "and he can be trusted."

"I have his cell phone number," I said. "I'll call him."

"I'll stand guard," Giovanna said. "I don't want Carlotta listening in."

Giovanna stood outside the door to the kitchen, while I walked to the far side of the room and punched in Franco's cell phone number.

Franco answered on the third ring.

When I told him what we wanted, he said he'd be there in a couple of minutes because he was already back in Como.

The three of us hurried to our rooms, packed a few things we thought we might need. Giovanna said there was already snow at that altitude.

As we headed back downstairs, Carlotta was pretending to sweep the carpets in the hallway, so I casually said, "It'll be nice to get to Milan, so we can finally do some shopping!"

"That's what I'm all about," Bess added, as if on cue. I didn't know whether Carlotta would believe us or not, but I was hoping that our real destination would never enter her mind.

11

Back at the Chalet . . .

Franco **was just pulling** up in front when we got downstairs, but this time he was driving a small sports car. I wasn't quite sure I wanted to be on winding mountain roads in that, but I figured we didn't have a choice.

The three of us hugged Giovanna, and for Carlotta's benefit said that we'd bring her back something nice from Milan. Then we jumped into Franco's sports car.

Franco must have been reading my mind, because he said, "I thought an SUV would give away where we were headed. We'll make a quick stop at my place and change vehicles."

"I'm relieved," I told him.

It didn't take us long to reach Franco's apartment, and the four of us piled into an SUV that looked like it could make it up any mountain.

"Ready?" Franco said.

"Ready!" the three of us replied.

With that, we started north toward Sondrio. For what seemed like forever, we paralleled the long lake, gradually climbing and getting into forest thick with pine trees.

When we finally reached Sondrio, we started through a valley called Malenco.

"It's fourteen miles deep and thirteen miles wide." Franco pointed to one of the peaks. "This is where I learned to ski."

Finally we reached the village of Chiareggio. Farther up was the massive Mount Disgrazia, which Franco told us was 12,100 feet high.

"See that little speck up there?" Franco asked.

The three of us squinted in the direction Franco was pointing.

"That's the chalet."

"Where's the road?" George asked.

"There is no road. There's only a trail for the cows and it's covered with snow, but it's all we need," Franco said. "I know where it is. We'll make it."

We drove a few miles farther up the road, then

Franco turned off abruptly, and we began bumping our way along the side of the snow-covered peak.

It was bone jarring, I've got to say, but Franco seemed to be in complete control. Most of the way up, all four wheels were never on the ground at the same time, and there were several times that I honestly thought the SUV would tip over. It wasn't long until our ears began to pop.

"Don't look back," Bess said.

Naturally I did. "Oh, wow!" I said.

The road we had been on looked like a thin silver thread. I had no idea we had really climbed that high and that far. Now the chalet was more visible, although the closer we got, the more Giovanna's description of it fit. It really did look as though it was about to fall down. That would be some end to our trip, if right when we were about to solve the mystery, the chalet collapsed on top of us!

As we made the final approach to the chalet, I thought about what it must have been like during that winter of 1944 for Princess Teresa-Maria and her family and Julius Mahoney. I hoped the solution to this mystery was somewhere within that sad-looking house.

Finally we reached the chalet, and Franco pulled the SUV in front.

"I'll get a fire started," Franco said. "There's a knapsack of food in the back. We won't starve while we're here."

I looked at Bess and George. The three of us were thinking the same thing—that we hadn't been thinking. I guess we just thought if we got hungry we'd run down the road to the nearest store.

"Thanks, Franco," I told him. "We're glad you're here."

"Well, I am too, if what we're doing will mean that Prince Carlo is no longer in trouble." Franco's face tightened, and I thought for a minute that we were going to have an angry outburst from him, but instead he grabbed the knapsack from the back and trudged up the front steps.

He opened the door without unlocking anything, so I decided that the royal family was either very trusting or the door was broken. Once inside, I saw that there were several cots arranged around the edge of the room.

When Franco saw me looking at the cots, he said, "The local farmers stay here sometimes in the early spring or early fall, when they're on the mountain, tending their herds, and a freak snowstorm comes up. The princess lets them do that, in return for helping to take care of the place."

Bess look around and raised an eyebrow.

"Well, they don't do a lot to take care of it, I guess," Franco agreed, "but at least nobody seems to bother it."

"That's good for us," I said. "That means we may still be able to find the letter that Prince Enzo wrote."

"Where do we start?" Bess was looking around for possible hiding places. "I don't want to move too many boards or stones, because I might just move the one that holds this place up."

"That's what I was thinking too," George agreed.

"It's still sturdy, though," Franco told us as he lit the fire, and stood back while it began to crackle. "These places were built to last for centuries."

I decided we'd have to take him at his word. "Do you mind if we start snooping around?" I said. "The sooner we start our search, the better off we'll be."

"I know," Franco said. "That's fine. I'll start putting together something to eat. Call me if you need me."

As we started up the staircase, I thought of something. I turned and looked at Franco. "Did Prince Enzo have a study here or was there one room in particular where he spent most of his time?"

Franco thought for a minute. "I don't know," he

said. "I don't think anybody ever mentioned that."

We continued up the staircase toward the second floor. Why would Prince Enzo have written this letter in the first place? I wondered. That was an important question that needed to be answered.

We reached a landing with a window that was cracked, letting in some of the cold air. I shivered.

"What a view," George said.

"It's gorgeous," Bess agreed, "but I'd hate to be caught in a blizzard up here. You're so far from anything—you could freeze to death."

I suddenly felt as if somebody had hit me over the head with a piece of important information. "That's it!" I exclaimed.

Bess and George looked at me. "What?" they asked in unison.

"That's why Prince Enzo wrote the letter," I told them. "I should have seen it. What he did was totally out of character, but when do people do things totally out of character? When they're confronted with situations they might not get out of."

"I don't see where you're going with this," George said.

"In 1944 Julius Mahoney helped the royal family move their most treasured belongings up here to keep them safe from the Fascists," I explained. "While they were here, a blizzard struck, and Prince Enzo thought he might not make it out alive, that they all might freeze to death."

Bess was nodding. "Faced with that," she added, "he wrote a letter, sort of like a last will and testament, in which he mentioned the help Julius Mahoney had given them, hoping that the letter would be found when everyone was discovered *and he would come off like a caring human being.*"

I nodded. "A lasting legacy."

"Why did he hide it then?" George asked. "Why didn't he just leave it out in the open?"

"When the weather broke, and Prince Enzo realized they would survive after all, he probably got greedy again," I said. "It happens all the time. People soften when they're faced with danger, but when things turn around and they realize they're going to make it after all, they sort of forget all the promises they made to themselves and to others."

Bess and George nodded.

"Princess Teresa-Maria knew about the letter, so Prince Enzo didn't think he could destroy it," I said. "So he probably convinced her that it would be safer if he just hid the letter until after the war was over. That way people couldn't accuse Julius Mahoney of collaborating with the enemy. I'm inferring a lot of this—we need to find that letter—but it makes sense."

"Why would they accuse him of that?" Bess asked.

"The Italians were our enemies during World War Two," I said. "I'm sure somebody would have been able to make something out of that. Let's look around."

There were four rooms upstairs. They were still furnished, although everything was covered with dust and what looked like the remains of some birds' nests. Nowhere did we find anywhere that a letter could be hidden.

"Are you hungry?" Franco called from downstairs.

"I am!" Bess shouted back.

"Me too!" George chimed in.

It must have been the air, because my stomach started making noises at the mention of food.

The three of us went back downstairs. It was now pleasantly warm—Franco had a wonderful fire going.

"That is a beautiful fireplace," Bess said. "I love fireplaces made out of natural stone."

"If you can believe this," Franco said, "Prince Enzo himself built this fireplace."

That raised our eyebrows.

Could it be possible? I wondered. "He doesn't

sound like the kind of person who'd enjoy physical labor," I said.

"Well, that's all he did here," Franco said. "The rest of it was done by local laborers."

I walked over to the fire and held my hands out to warm them. The fireplace was almost a work of art, and it made me wonder what else Prince Enzo could have done, if he had worried less about achieving great wealth and more about living a good life. Some of the stones had separated from their masonry, and several of them looked loose, as though they could be taken out.

While Bess and George began helping themselves to the food that Franco had set out, I began to jiggle some of the stones. The first three moved slightly but stayed where they were when I tried to remove them. The fourth stone, near the bottom right-hand side, came out with just a little effort.

My heart was almost in my mouth as I put my hand in the space and began feeling around. Suddenly I touched what felt like an envelope. I slowly pulled it out and looked at it. On the front, in very ornate handwriting, was a message in Italian. Slowly, carefully, I managed to translate the fairly simple words: *In the event of my death, please open.* It was signed by Prince Enzo.

12

Princess Teresa-Maria's Secret

I **scanned the letter quickly,** just to make sure it was what Princess Teresa-Maria had mentioned in her diary. Then I opened my mouth to tell everyone the good news, but I closed it just as fast when a cell phone rang.

I saw Franco pull his cell phone out of his pocket, look at the screen, then turn away to answer it.

Bess and George were busy filling their plates and weren't paying any attention to what Franco was saying, and I was too far away to hear.

Suddenly something told me to keep quiet—my sixth sense, I guess—so I slipped the letter inside my jacket and quickly replaced the stone in the fireplace.

I didn't think anybody had really paid any attention to what I was doing. For all they knew, I had simply been warming my hands by the fire.

I walked over to Bess and George as nonchalantly as I could. As with most people in a similar situation, I was sure that my face betrayed what I was thinking, but when Bess looked up and saw me, all she said was, "Get some food, Nancy. Everything is delicious."

"It does look wonderful," I told her.

I began filling up a paper plate, but out of the corner of my left eye I was watching Franco as he continued to talk on his cell phone. He seemed to be arguing with someone about something. Was he talking to Prince Paolo? Were they trying to decide the best way to get rid of us once we discovered the letter? I suddenly wondered if the chills I was feeling were because of the weather or because I had led us into a trap. There might be three of us, but I knew we'd be no match for a man who could have competed for the title of Mr. Universe!

I didn't know if I could force any of the food down my throat, but I had to act as if everything was normal, so I took a bite and began chewing slowly.

It was good, so that helped, but as I was eating I

noticed that Franco—still on his cell—glanced in my direction several times. That made it difficult to swallow.

Suddenly Franco stopped talking and said, "Nancy! Could you please come here a minute?"

I almost choked on an olive, but I managed to say, "All right."

Bess and George, who still seemed oblivious to the danger we might be in, both winked at me.

Under her breath Bess whispered, "Lucky!"

Yeah, right! I wanted to say. Well, the minute he tried anything, I'd use every martial arts move I knew!

I stood up and started to where Franco was leaning against the wall. Then it occurred to me that maybe Dad had been kidnapped and they were holding him for ransom, until we either gave up the search of the letter or gave it to Prince Paolo when we found it.

I needed to remain calm. I took a deep breath and slowly let it out. When I reached Franco, I said, "What's wrong?"

"Will you please talk to Gina for me?" Franco said. "She thinks I'm seeing you behind her back!"

I gave him a puzzled look. "What?"

"It's Gina on the phone, my fiancée," Franco

explained. "She thinks that I want to break off our engagement and start seeing you."

I couldn't help it. I laughed out loud. "Okay," I said, taking the cell phone from him. "Hello, Gina?"

For the next few minutes I talked to Gina Poppi, and finally convinced her that I had no designs on Franco. Gina turned out to be a really charming girl and ended up inviting us to her wedding in Venice in a couple of months.

When I hung up, Bess and George starting teasing Franco mercilessly about taking three girls to a mountain chalet when he was engaged.

"You should have brought her along," George said. "We'd love to meet her."

"Ah!" Franco said, feigning frustration. "She and her mother are too busy with wedding preparations."

"Oh, I'd love to see her gown," Bess said. "I'm sure it's beautiful!"

Franco grunted, and we all laughed again.

I felt so guilty about not trusting Franco that I just blurted out, "Well, I found the letter!"

There was stunned silence for a minute, then everyone, including Franco, cheered.

"Problem is, I don't know much Italian." I mentally kicked myself for not bringing along an

Italian dictionary. "Franco, would you mind translating for us?"

While we all finished eating, Franco gave us a rough idea of what the letter said. Julius Mahoney, an American soldier who was stationed at the German-Italian line, helped the royal family recover their most important belongings from a local Fascist leader, then secreted them away in the family's mountain chalet. Princess Teresa-Maria had told Prince Enzo that she wanted to repay Julius Mahoney and his family for all his help. She had noticed him admiring one of the paintings they had brought to the chalet, and she wanted to give it to him. She could tell that he had no intention of taking it, like some soldiers on both sides had done. And if it hadn't been for him, they would have nothing.

Prince Enzo wrote that he agreed with Princess Teresa-Maria that it would be a fitting gift to the American officer, and that when they were able to make arrangements after the war, they would send it to him in River Heights, provided they survived the blizzard. This was all the evidence we needed to prove that Prince Carlo was telling the truth.

But we were also in for a surprise. I had actually wondered if there might be something else behind the gift, and that was in the letter too. Prince Enzo admitted that he believed his wife, Princess Teresa-Maria, had fallen in love with the American officer. He knew that it was only at a distance, but he could tell by her eyes. He didn't fault Princess Teresa-Maria, saying that their marriage had been arranged, as was the tradition then in the royal family, and that he didn't think he had been a very good husband. He ended the letter by saying that if he had only had another chance, he would change his ways and be a better husband and father.

I looked up from the letter. "Of course, as we know now, he was given another chance," I said, "but he obviously didn't change his ways."

"Not at all," Franco said.

Since it was already dark, Franco suggested that we stay in the chalet until first light, so it would be easier going back down the mountain.

"Of course, I know my way in the dark," Franco added, "so if you want to go on, we can—"

"Oh, no!" Bess said. "I think we should stay here!"

"I've never spent the night in a mountain chalet," George chimed in. "It'll be a first."

I agreed with them, although I knew that all three of us were thinking about the many horrible things that could happen if we tried to maneuver the SUV down a boulder-strewn, snow-covered mountain in the dark.

As it turned out, Franco spent most of the night talking to Gina on his cell phone. Well, actually, Gina did all the talking and Franco slept, waking up from time to time to grunt, *"Si, si, comprendo, cara mia!"*

We were all sure he hadn't understood a word, but it seemed to satisfy Gina.

Bess, George, and I dozed from time to time, stirring only when we heard Franco banking the fire so it wouldn't go out.

All three of us were mostly awake early the next morning when Franco said, "I'll take care of the embers in the fireplace, if the three of you want to go ahead and get in the SUV." He handed me the keys. "Why don't you start it, Nancy, so it'll be warm when I get inside?"

I laughed. "Thanks, Franco."

The trip down the mountain was like a roller-coaster ride, although never once did I think we were in danger. Franco was an amazing driver.

Just as we neared the turn off to Cernobbio, Franco's cell phone rang. It was Giovanna. During the night Franco had called her and told her about the discovery of the letter. Now Giovanna wanted us to go straight to the hospital in Milan to Princess Teresa-Maria. She was much better, and her doctors said she could visit with us—something she wanted to do very much. Dad would be there too. Giovanna had already arranged for the rest of our belongings to be taken to the hospital, since we would be leaving the next morning for River Heights.

As we entered Milan, I was reminded once again of what an amazing city it is, and I began to wish that we could have spent some time there. There was so much to see and do. Another time, I decided.

The hospital was on the Via Alessandro Manzoni. Franco told us that it was a private hospital and that it had once been the residence of Italian royalty. He drove through the front gate, and we parked at the rear of the courtyard.

Princess Teresa-Maria's room was on the third floor. Dad was standing outside, talking to a nursing sister, but when he saw us, he excused himself and hurried up to us.

"Giovanna told me the good news," Dad said. "I'm glad one of us was lucky."

"What do you mean?" I asked.

"I've been dealing with various bureaucracies since I got here, Nancy," Dad explained. "I basically got nowhere." He shook his head. "I'm glad this won't go to trial, because it would have been a legal nightmare."

I took out the letter and gave it to Dad. "Here's all

the evidence you'll need to clear Prince Carlo."

Dad took the letter and put it inside his briefcase. "Once I get a sworn statement from Princess Teresa-Maria, basically saying that this is Prince Enzo's handwriting and that she agrees with the contents in the letter, then we can fly back to River Heights."

It suddenly occurred to me that Princess Teresa-Maria might not want to agree with the part of the letter in which her husband claimed that she had fallen in love with Julius Mahoney, but I was wrong.

"Of course, it's all true, every bit of it," Princess Teresa-Maria said in a strong voice. "I'll sign whatever you want me to sign."

Dad had already drafted a statement to that effect, so, while we all watched, Prince Carlo's great-grandmother signed the document with a flourish, and then said, "Now, return my great-grandson to me as soon as possible. He has work to do."

We all knew that she was talking about Prince Carlo's becoming head of the royal family. With all that had happened since we had been here, especially the behavior of Prince Paolo, I knew there was no doubt that whatever Princess Teresa-Maria wanted, Princess Teresa-Maria would get.

But she was still a great-grandmother who wanted

us to sit by her bed so she could tell us how wonderful her great-grandson, Prince Carlo, was.

So we did.

We also put together more pieces of the puzzle. Princess Teresa-Maria actually had kept in touch with Julius Mahoney, but she had asked him to destroy her letters and she had destroyed his.

"We were just friends," Princess Teresa-Maria said, "but I was sure my family would think there was more to it than that, so I didn't want to give them anything to use against me."

"So that's why I didn't find any letters from you in Julius Mahoney's things," I said. "He kept his promise to you."

Princess Teresa-Maria was hearing this for the first time, I knew, and it made her smile. "He was a remarkable man, Nancy," she said. "He really was."

Princess Teresa-Maria's stories weren't the creation of a deteriorating mental state, as some of the relatives had claimed. She was quite in command of her senses.

"Prince Carlo will be so happy to hear all of this," I told her, squeezing her hand. "I can hardly wait to tell him."

Princess Teresa-Maria squeezed back. "Thank you, Nancy Drew," she whispered.

13

A Royal Wedding

I was *so* **ready to** get back to River Heights. Dad had already talked to everybody, including Prince Carlo, the FBI director, the Attorney General, and the Italian ambassador to the United States. They all seemed pleased that the matter was over, and that an international incident had been avoided.

"I think you might have missed somebody," I told Dad.

He gave me a puzzled look. "Really?" he said. "Who?"

"The president of the United States," I replied with a grin.

Dad rolled his eyes. "I'm sure he knows about it," he said. "All charges have been dropped against

Prince Carlo, and he's a free man. In fact, you'll probably see him at the airport, because he said he was going to be there when we arrived."

It would be good to see Prince Carlo in person to tell him what Princess Teresa-Maria had said.

The jet touched down smoothly and taxied to Gate 1. For just a minute I had a sense of déjà vu. It hadn't really been all that long since Prince Carlo had been doing exactly what we were doing now, but a million different things had happened since, and his life had been an emotional roller coaster. I knew he must be glad that things were finally getting back to normal—well, as normal as things can be for an Italian prince.

The pilot expertly parked the plane, and within minutes we had grabbed our carry-ons and Bess, George, and I were hurrying down the gangway.

When we reached the end of the passageway and could see into the waiting area, the three of us stopped, stunned by what was in front of us.

Mrs. Mahoney and Prince Carlo were there, but standing next to Prince Carlo was Jocylin Ross's niece, Sophia.

"It's the girl from the gallery," Bess said.

"You're right!" George said. "Why does Prince Carlo have his arm around her?"

All of a sudden the final piece of the puzzle fell into place. "Well, well, well," I said. "Now it all makes sense."

Bess and George looked at me. "It does?" they said in unison.

I nodded. "Come on," I told them. "Let's go give the couple our congratulations."

When we reached Prince Carlo and Sophia, he surprised us all with hugs instead of formal handshakes, ignoring any royal formalities that might have been lingering. Mrs. Mahoney joined in, so all of a sudden, we were almost like family.

"Thank you so much, Nancy," Prince Carlo said. "There is no way I can ever repay you."

"The painting is already in the River Heights Art Gallery," Mrs. Mahoney said. "The formal presentation will take place in a couple of weeks. I've invited art historians and critics from all over to country to be there."

Prince Carlo turned to Sophia. "I think you've already met the mystery artist," he said with a huge smile. "I caught her red-handed putting some of her sketches on the porch of your house."

"So you're the one!" Bess gasped.

Sophia smiled. "I'm the one."

Dad had joined us now. "Let's go home," he said.

As we left the gate area Dad filled in the legal details for Prince Carlo, while Sophia told us why she had secretly left her artwork at our house.

"When I was in Italy, I met Princess Teresa-Maria at a gallery opening," Sophia said. "It was one of those immediate connections. I didn't even know at first she was a princess, until she told me that her great-grandson, Prince Carlo, was an artist, and would love to see my work. Well, I was floored and was just sure that a prince wouldn't be interested in me at all.

"But I began to attend his shows, to study his paintings, and I even talked to him a couple of times, although I never let him know that his great-grandmother had suggested that I show him my work. I fell in love with both him and his art.

"When my parents died, I came to River Heights to live with my aunt, and I just couldn't believe it when Prince Carlo arrived to donate the painting to the River Heights Art Museum.

"When I learned that he would be staying with the Drews while he awaited the outcome of his legal situation, I decided to show him my work—anonymously. I don't know what I really expected, nothing, probably, except the knowledge that he had at least finally seen my work. That would have been enough in itself, but then he caught me." Sophia gave us a big smile. "I'm sure a psychologist would say I wanted to be found out."

"I'm sure he or she would," I told her, "but who cares?"

"That's what I'm saying." Bess glanced back at Prince Carlo. "I saw how he looked at you, Sophia. You're going to be a princess soon!"

When we arrived home from the airport, there were still a lot of people in front of our house, but now they were carrying signs that said LONG LIVE CARLO AND SOPHIA.

"These people need to get a life," Bess muttered.

"This is their life," George told her. "They enjoy living vicariously through other people."

When I stepped out of our car, a reporter stuck a microphone in my face and said, "You got Prince Carlo off the hook, Ms. Drew. Would you care to tell our viewers how you did it?"

I knew it was useless to do anything except give him some kind of a comment, so I let him know that Prince Carlo had been telling the truth, that evidence was found in a letter from his great-grandfather, corroborating his story, and that the rest would probably come out eventually from

Prince Carlo, but that I didn't feel it was my place to give any more information about it.

That seemed to satisfy the reporter, because he pulled the microphone away from my face, and said, "Thank you!"

Inside we found Ned in the kitchen, having just finished preparing us a light lunch.

"Where's Han . . . ," I started to ask, but at that moment Hannah came into the kitchen and said, "Nancy, your boyfriend is a really good cook!"

I grinned at Ned. "I'll remember that."

For the first few minutes at the table, Ned's untapped talent in the kitchen was the main topic of conversation, but it soon gave way to the end of Prince Carlo's story.

"Princess Teresa-Maria called me this morning," Prince Carlo told us. "When I get back to Italy, she's going to call all of the family together and name me the head."

"Can she really do that?" George asked.

Prince Carlo nodded. "If I'm put in charge of her estate in her will," he explained, "I'll oversee the family fortune."

"I can't imagine anyone more suited to do that than you, Prince Carlo," Dad said.

"I appreciate the faith you have in me, Mr. Drew,"

Prince Carlo said. "It'll be a daunting task, trying to keep the family from self-destructing, but I think I can do it." He turned to Sophia. "With your help," he added.

For the first time Sophia blushed.

"Are you telling me that a royal wedding is in the future?" I asked.

Prince Carlo nodded. "I also talked to Princess Teresa-Maria about that this morning," he said. "She remembered Sophia, and she's delighted that she'll be joining the family."

Bess turned to me. "Well, Nancy, with a royal wedding coming up, we need to start on your wardrobe right now," she said. "I will not accompany you to Italy unless you plan to make heads turn in Milan."

"Like that'll happen," I told her.

Still, I was willing to give up my comfortable clothes for the chance to attend a royal wedding. I didn't want to put a jinx on anything for Prince Carlo and Sophia, but I couldn't imagine anything more fun than a royal wedding—*with a mystery*. Who knew? It could happen.

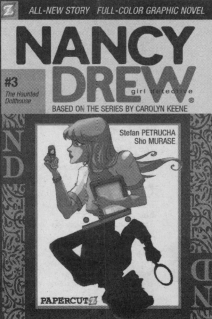

REDISCOVER THE CLASSIC MYSTERIES OF NANCY DREW

$5.99 ($8.99 CAN) each
AVAILABLE AT YOUR LOCAL BOOKSTORE OR LIBRARY

Grosset & Dunlap • A division of Penguin Young Readers Group
A member of Penguin Group (USA), Inc. • A Pearson Company
www.penguin.com/youngreaders

HAVE YOU READ ALL OF THE ALICE BOOKS?

PHYLLIS REYNOLDS NAYLOR

STARTING WITH ALICE
Atheneum Books for
  Young Readers
  0-689-84395-X
Aladdin Paperbacks
  0-689-84396-8

ALICE IN BLUNDERLAND
Atheneum Books for
  Young Readers
  0-689-84397-6

LOVINGLY ALICE
Atheneum Books for
  Young Readers
  0-689-84399-2

THE AGONY OF ALICE
Atheneum Books for
  Young Readers
  0-689-31143-5
Aladdin Paperbacks
  0-689-81672-3

ALICE IN RAPTURE,
  SORT-OF
Atheneum Books for
  Young Readers
  0-689-31466-3
Aladdin Paperbacks
  0-689-81687-1

RELUCTANTLY ALICE
Atheneum Books for
  Young Readers
  0-689-31681-X
Aladdin Paperbacks
  0-689-81688-X

ALL BUT ALICE
Atheneum Books for
Young Readers
  0-689-31773-5
Aladdin Paperbacks
  0-689-85044-1

ALICE IN APRIL
Atheneum Books for
  Young Readers
  0-689-31805-7
Aladdin Paperbacks
  0-689-81686-3

ALICE IN-BETWEEN
Atheneum Books for
  Young Readers
  0-689-31890-0
Aladdin Paperbacks
  0-689-81685-5

ALICE THE BRAVE
Atheneum Books for
  Young Readers
  0-689-80095-9
Aladdin Paperbacks
  0-689-80598-5

ALICE IN LACE
Atheneum Books for
  Young Readers
  0-689-80358-3
Aladdin Paperbacks
  0-689-80597-7

OUTRAGEOUSLY ALICE
Atheneum Books for
  Young Readers
  0-689-80354-0
Aladdin Paperbacks
  0-689-80596-9

ACHINGLY ALICE
Atheneum Books for
  Young Readers
  0-689-80533-9
Aladdin Paperbacks
  0-689-80595-0
Simon Pulse
  0-689-86396-9

ALICE ON THE OUTSIDE
Atheneum Books for
  Young Readers
  0-689-80359-1
Simon Pulse
  0-689-80594-2

GROOMING OF ALICE
Atheneum Books for
  Young Readers
  0-689-82633-8
Simon Pulse
  0-689-84618-5

ALICE ALONE
Atheneum Books for
  Young Readers
  0-689-82634-6
Simon Pulse
  0-689-85189-8

SIMPLY ALICE
Atheneum Books for
  Young Readers
  0-689-84751-3
Simon Pulse
  0-689-85965-1

PATIENTLY ALICE
Atheneum Books for
  Young Readers
  0-689-82636-2
Simon Pulse
  0-689-87073-6

INCLUDING ALICE
Atheneum Books for
  Young Readers
  0-689-82637-0

Think it would be fun to get stuck on a deserted island with the guy you sort of like? Well, try adding the girl who gets on your nerves big-time (*and* who's crushing on the same guy), the bossiest kid in school, your annoying little brother, and a bunch of other people, all of whom have their own ideas about how things should be done. Oh, and have I mentioned that there's no way off this island, and no one knows where you are?

Still sound great? Didn't think so.

Now all I have to worry about is getting elected island leader, finding something to wear for a dance (if you can believe that), and surviving a hurricane, all while keeping my crush away from Little Miss Priss. Oh, and one other teeny-tiny little thing: surviving.

Get me outta here!

Read all the books in the Castaways trilogy:

#1 Worst Class Trip Ever

#2 Weather's Here, Wish You Were Great

#3 Isle Be Seeing You